MCR
Gift

MCR

OCT 3 0 2006

EVANSTON PUBLIC LIBRARY

3 1192 01334 2181

J Bugbe.M
Bugbee, M. Howe.
Beyond the road /

DATE DUE

JUL 0 9 2007

NOV 0 5 2007

D1161859

DEMCO, INC. 38-2931

Beyond the Road

✱ ✱ ✱ ✱ ✱ ✱ ✱

Beyond the Road

✳ ✳ ✳ ✳ ✳ ✳

M. Howe Bugbee

Mayhaven Publishing

EVANSTON PUBLIC LIBRARY
CHILDREN'S DEPARTMENT
1703 ORRINGTON AVENUE
EVANSTON, ILLINOIS 60201

Mayhaven Publishing
PO Box 557
Mahomet, IL 61853
USA

All rights reserved.
No part of this book may be reproduced or transmitted in any form
or by any means without written permission from the publisher,
except for the inclusion of brief quotations in a review.

Cover Art: Jean Spencer

Copyright © 2006

First Edition—First Printing 2006

1 2 3 4 5 6 7 8 9 10

LOC: 2005923128
ISBN-13 978-193227808-8
ISBN 1932278-08-7

Printed in Canada

Special Thanks

The author wishes to express sincere gratitude to story-teller, historian, educator, and writer Joseph M. Marshall III, recipient of the Wyoming Humanities Award, and author of *The Lakota Way, On Behalf of the Wolf and the First Peoples, The Dance House, Winter of the Holy Iron, Soldiers Falling into Camp,* and *The Journey of Crazy Horse* for reading the manuscript for Lakota accuracy. The author has the utmost respect for Marshall's work, his benevolence with his time, and his dedication to his people and the craft of writing. He never wavered when asked to read the manuscript or when asked numerous questions regarding the Lakota language and culture. Many, many thanks.

Acknowledgements

Special thanks to Lou Eliopulos, former Chief Forensic Investigator for the Jacksonville Sheriff's Office, Jacksonville, Florida, and author of *Death Investigator's Handbook,* for advice regarding the medical examiner. Thanks also to David M. Cressler, General Manager, OHC Environmental Engineering, Jacksonville, Florida for a mini course on toxic wastes.

Many others provided support and encouragement. My husband, Walter Bugbee, never hesitated when asked to listen to the same chapter over again. His time, patience and support are resolute. My friend Kathy Mixson read and edited many versions, tolerated my obsessions over single words, and never wavered when asked to read another. She truly is a Goddess.

Thanks to many including: Sisters in Crime and the Bard Society for their critiques and insights; my family and friends for encouragement; my teachers Frank Green and Jim Frey for their wisdom and insights; my sons, Marc and Alex, for their support, suggestions and patience; Charles Dunn for teaching me about Indian artifacts as well as local history and euphemisms; Sharon Morgan, Levy Schroeder, and Ginger Cheek for years of encouragement and feedback; Doris Wenzel and her staff at Mayhaven Publishing for selecting the book for publication; Eden Kuhlenschmidt, Kay Heil and their students at River Valley Middle School, Jeffersonville, Indiana, who read and critiqued the story.

✻ ✻ ✻ ✻ ✻ ✻

"We Lakota believe there are many roads in life, but that there are two that are most important: the Red Road and the Black Road. They represent the two perspectives to every situation, the two sides of every person, the two choices we frequently face in life. The Red Road is the good way, the good side, and the right choice. It is a narrow road fraught with dangers and obstacles and is extremely difficult to travel. The Black Road is the bad way, the bad side, the wrong choice. It is wide and very easy to travel. The Red Road and the Black Road appear in many of our stories, not as roads but as the personifications of right and wrong, good and bad, light and dark."

From *The Lakota Way* by Joseph M. Marshall, copyright (c) 2001 by Joseph M. Marshall III. Used by permission of Viking Penguin, a division of Penguin Group (USA) Inc

Table of Contents

Bridgeport	11
Missing	13
Grave Discovery	26
Tell-Tale Scar	35
A Killer in Bridgeport	42
The Body Detective	45
Instant Celebrity	56
The Big Stink	68
Pythagorus	78
What Goes Around...	89
Moonlight Chase	104
Only a Fool is Fearless	114
Telling the Truth	121
Witness Tattooed on his Forehead	128
Unfamiliar Territory	139
A Killer Gets Close	146
What Are Friends For?	155
Who's Watching Robin?	160
A Pint-Sized Witness	168
Two and Two Make Four	174
The *Real* Bad Boy	197
A Nose for Money	203
On the Run	208
The Long Night	227
The Attack	249
A Spider to the Rescue	264
On The Edge	270
A Special Kind of Courage	283
Glossary	286
Resources	288

Bridgeport
✳ ✳ ✳ ✳ ✳ ✳

Bridgeport, Indiana, is a postage stamp of a town with a sticky past. A town nestled in a bend of the Ohio River that harbors high bluffs and homes linked by winding country roads. It is usually a tranquil place with a cornfield tapestry that exudes a loamy aroma of earth and corn. Yet at its edge are fields and woods inhabited by shadows that seem to shuffle whispering ghosts of long ago.

Like the state, Bridgeport's roots are Indian, but the natives migrated with the buffalo and Caucasians moved in. Soon after, river pirates chose Bridgeport for their lair so they could plunder along the Ohio and then disappear into the rugged land like rain. When the town chased the pirates away, it flourished, and today is like a tulip that has risen from a dark winter.

Still, every quarter century or so, an upside-down crescent moon appears and something vile happens. Storytellers say as the pirates left, they slashed open the sky over Bridgeport, creating a portal for their return. Old timers recognize the cosmic warning and lock their windows and doors and stay inside. The young, and those new to Bridgeport, will learn to do the same—if they survive.

Missing
✳ ✳ ✳ ✳ ✳ ✳

Through the kitchen window, thirteen-year-old Robin Beekler watched charcoal clouds rolling over Seth Dyer's cornfield like giant, billowy tumbleweeds. She thought about the weird moon she'd seen the night before and how, when she talked about it at breakfast, her stepfather told her to get a 900 number and a turban to tell fortunes. It had not been a fun meal. They rarely were with Stanley Edwards around.

She shifted her weight from one bare foot to the other while scrubbing an egg-encrusted plate. As she rinsed the dish, Stanley's voice boomed behind her.

"My grandmother can wash dishes faster than that, and she's eighty-five. Stop daydreaming and get the job done."

"I'm thinking," she said, "besides, why are you always on my case?"

"Just wait till you get out in the real world, kid." He drank from the orange juice carton. Juice dribbled down his

13

chin and he wiped it with the back of his hand.

She winced, vowing never to drink orange juice again.

"When you're standing on an assembly for eight to ten hours at a stretch, you'll see what work is really like. Just try to complain then."

He spun her around by the shoulders. "And look at me when I talk to you."

Her eyes rolled up to his unshaven face and dark, narrowed eyes. "I'd be done by now if you'd leave me alone."

He pointed a finger in her face. "If one of my men at the factory talked to me like that he'd be gone. Just like that." He snapped two fingers. "He'd be history."

She pressed her lips together to cage the angry words filling her mouth.

"You're nothing but a spoiled brat," he said. "And ya sure ain't blessed with looks, either." He shook his head. "You're pathetic with those glasses and all that wiry red hair sticking out all over the place. And all this honor roll stuff you tell your mother—I know it's a bunch of bologna 'cause you sure don't use your head around here."

That was it! She stepped away from the sink and hurled the rag into the water, splashing suds onto the curtain and window.

"I make straight A's." She looked at his protruding stomach. "And I wouldn't talk about somebody's looks if I were you."

His pasty complexion reddened. He reached for her, but she darted for the front door, hitting it with the flat of her hand. It flung open, narrowly missing her mother coming up the steps with groceries. The tall, slender woman spun around, causing a lock of her hair to flip into her eyes. She blew it off her face as she peered over the brown bag.

"Sorry, Mom," Robin called, stutter-stepping down the porch steps.

"Honey, where are you going?"

"As far away from him as I can get." She jerked the handlebars of her old Murray bike propped against the house and guided it across the grass toward the road.

Her mother started down the steps. "Honey, what's wrong? Where are you going?"

Through clenched teeth, Robin said, "I don't know."

"That's not good enough, young lady."

"Seth's, I guess. He won't hassle me."

Her mother sat down on the bottom step as the bike bumped over the curb and rolled onto the road.

Robin jumped on and pedaled angrily until her calves ached. When she was far enough from her house on Maple Road, she plopped down on the bike seat to rest. As the bike rolled along she thought of her mother who used to be fun till she married Stanley, and got her promotion at the bank. Now she was tired and cranky all the time.

She thought about the argument over the upside-down

moon and how Stanley had made fun of her, even though her mother found an article about it in the newspaper. The article told about a pirate curse and about wicked happenings that coincided with its appearance. Stanley tossed the paper into the trash and her mother had bailed out by going to the store, leaving Robin to clean up and listen to him rant.

As she pedaled, she pushed her loose, horn-rimmed glasses back up on her skinny nose. The frames had broken when they tangled in her hair and fell to the pavement. Cheap ol' Stanley glued them together instead of buying new ones. She hated them. She also hated her hair and the way it always flopped into her face like a stringy mop. She hated many things right now, but couldn't do much about any of them.

She drew in a breath to clear her head and the wind brushed her cheeks. Being outside made her feel much better. All of nature, her Lakota friend had told her, makes one feel connected. With the way things were at home, that's exactly what she needed. Going to Seth's would also help. He would be glad to see her. He always was. She never told him, but in her heart he was her pretend grandfather.

The sun was barely visible in a soup of clouds, but through an opening she saw the outline of the upside-down crescent moon. She was mesmerized till leaves tumbled across the road like little brown kites, drawing her attention back to the pavement and the chilly wind. She tucked the tail of her flannel shirt in her jeans and pulled the sleeves down over her fingers.

Raindrops splattered her glasses making them as opaque as a frosted mug. If she were running the world, she would have someone make little windshield wipers for glasses. But for now, she was still a kid and couldn't do anything about it, so she yanked them off and stuffed them into her pocket. Then a gust of wind shoved the bike into the middle of the road. A branch smashed to the ground and skimmed across the road like a crab. She swerved, barely missing it. She knew she had to get to Seth's before things got worse.

She pedaled hard and within minutes her wheels crunched along his gravel driveway till she reached the house. She lifted the bike onto the porch and laid it flat so it wouldn't blow over. Inside, Rags, Seth's shaggy dog, barked. Seth was probably already heading for the door.

She pulled the glasses from her pocket, wiped them on her shirt as best she could, and slid them back on. When her eyes focused, she noticed four newspapers lying haphazardly on the porch. *Four?* Her stomach tightened like a fist. She quickly knocked on the front door and stepped back while she waited. The screen door rattled in the frame. Rags barked louder and jumped against the door.

"Seth?"

Rags moved to the picture window and barked. *Seth should have answered by now.* She framed her hands around her eyes and peered through the window. A light shone in the back of the house. She knocked louder, hurting her bony knuckles. *Was he in the bathroom? Had he fallen?*

The rain changed to hail and bombarded the porch. She flattened against the door and pounded it with her fist.

"Seth. Are you okay?" She pressed her ear to the door, trying to listen above the rain and wind. No response. She looked over her shoulder at the fields. *Surely he wouldn't be out there in the storm.*

Forsythia bushes raked the side of the house and Rags whined long and shrill. That was it. One way or another, she was going in.

"Hold on, Ragsy."

She turned the knob and, to her surprise, it opened. A gust of wind blew the door and banged it against the wall. She thrust out her hand to keep it from rebounding in her face. Rags jumped up and licked her face, causing her to stumble backwards. Then he raced down the steps into the rain and hail and hiked his leg at the first bush. She called out for Seth as she stepped inside, but when she glanced back at Rags, he was running up the drive.

She cupped her hands around her mouth and yelled, "Rags! Come here!"

He stopped and looked back.

"Here boy! Come on." She held her breath. The last thing she wanted was to chase him in that mess.

He lowered his head while hail pelted him and ricocheted onto the gravel. Slowly, he started for the house. She breathed a sigh of relief, till he stopped and looked back at the road.

"Come back!" she shouted.

He lowered his head and lumbered back to the porch.

"Good boy. Good boy. Is your daddy inside?"

He shook his soppy coat and licked her face when she bent down to pat him. His chocolate-brown eyes looked so sad. She wished he could talk.

"Come on. Let's look for Seth."

She grabbed his collar and coaxed him across the threshold. As soon as she did, a foul odor made her pinch her nose. She released Rags' collar, flipped on the light switch, and winced when she saw dog feces and urine at her feet. She started to step over the mess, but the wind slammed the door shut behind her, making her jump with fright and land in a mushy brown pile.

"Yuck!" She shook her foot and the stinky goo plopped to the floor. She hopped on one foot to the tissue box on the coffee table, grabbed several, and wiped the sole of her sneaker. She wasn't sure what to do with the soiled tissue, but finally dropped it on the pile. She could clean it up later after she found Seth.

Outside, the storm began to rage. Thunder rattled the windows. She hurried through the house calling his name, her wet sneakers squeaking across the floor. In the kitchen, she found a sack of dog food chewed open and brown nuggets scattered across the blue and white tile. At least Rags had gotten food. But the water dish was dry. She grimaced as she realized where he'd gotten his water and rubbed her face hard, wishing she hadn't let him lick her cheek.

Seth's house had two bedrooms and a bathroom down the hallway off the kitchen. She checked the bathroom and noticed Seth's bedroom door slightly ajar.

As she reached out to open it, Rags bounded past and knocked the door against the stop. She slumped against the wall to calm her nerves while he leapt onto the bed and walked like he was on a trampoline. Finally, he settled down and laid his head on the pillow.

The room was tidy, like Seth. His folded pajamas lay on the end of the bed. His glasses and Bible were on a small table nearby. On the dresser stood a picture of him with his arm around his wife who died years before. Though they were younger in the photograph, Robin could see the familiar scar on Seth's arm.

Lightning flashed through the lacy curtains, illuminating the space between the wall and the bed. She got the sinking feeling Seth might have fallen there. She didn't want to look, but knew she must.

She hurried across the room and forced herself to look

down, but there was nothing but beige carpet. She exhaled and leaned against the wall to figure out what to do next when something struck the window beside her. Her whole body tensed. She peeked around the curtain and saw a hole in the window screen about the size of a dime. Hanging from its barbed edge was a quivering black feather. A bird must have been confused by the storm.

She released the curtain and tried to think. *Where is he?* The only place left was the yard—and the cornfield. She charged through the kitchen and flung open the back door, knocking over a green metal bucket that banged all the way down the porch steps.

She caught her breath, then stepped onto the porch and yelled, "Seth!"

The wind whistled around the house and pushed her across the porch. At the wooden rail, she called his name again, but the rain pounded the word into the grass. She scanned the side yard and was surprised to see his tractor in the middle of the sunflower bed, crushing the ten-foot flowers like leafy stick figures. Seth would never drive the tractor into the flower bed. *Something was wrong, dead wrong.* It was time to call for help.

As she reached the screen door, something struck the back of her head. She ducked and raised her arms for protection as she turned to face her attacker.

Hovering just inches from her face was a black bird, a

crow, flapping its wings against the wind and looking bigger than any she'd ever seen. It cawed, then pecked at her.

She waved her arms wildly. "Go away! Shoooooo!"

It swooshed its wings and pecked again, hitting her flailing hand, acting as though it might fly right through her. Currents of feathered wind brushed her face.

She backed against the door, holding an arm up while she fished for the handle, opened it, and slipped behind the screen door. The crow tilted its head and watched with menacing, beady eyes. Then as quickly as it had appeared it swooped away, disappearing around the corner of the house.

Rags tried to get out, but she pushed him back and kicked the solid door closed. She dried her glasses with the kitchen towel and noticed a trickle of blood on the back of her right hand. She quickly ran hot water over it. It was nothing, although the vein looked swollen, but she'd had worse. *What was that crazy bird up to?* It must've been frightened or disoriented by the storm. That's all.

When she reached the living room, she snapped up the phone, but her shaky, wet finger paused over the keypad. She wasn't sure whom to call. Finally, she decided on Kota, her friend's grandfather. She knew his number, and since he was a good friend of Seth's he would know where he was or what to do.

She shivered and dripped cold drops onto the floor while punching in the numbers. As she waited, the phone seemed unusually quiet. She pressed the receiver harder against her ear, but it was silent. With petrified fingers, she jabbed the phone buttons, then realized the line was dead.

With the phone still against her ear, she wondered what to do. Then she thought something brushed her shoulder. She spun around, but didn't see anything. Something scraped in the dark corner by the door and Rags bared his teeth and growled. She gripped the receiver tighter and strained to see, but the corner was too dark.

Outside, branches raked the roof. Her eyes looked toward the ceiling. Lightning flashed, followed by an eerie cracking sound ripping the air, and a thundering crash shook the house, rattling the windows in their frames. The lights flickered once. Twice. She heard a 'zzz-zz-zzz' sound and the room went black.

Lowering the receiver into its cradle, she peered around the dark room and then back at the even darker corner. Her heart thumped loudly and her teeth chattered, telegraphing her to leave. Lightning flashed. In the brief light she saw Rags staring down the hall. She swallowed and backed toward Seth's easy chair.

Branches continued scraping the tin roof, grating her nerves. She rubbed her cold, wet arms and stared at the window of gray light as she wondered what to do. Somewhere up there was that moon—the one with the curse. She shrank into the oversized chair and patted the seat for Rags to jump up, which he quickly did. The smell of wet dog and the foul odor rising from the floor was almost overwhelming. Still, she'd rather put up with the stench than be alone in the storm.

"It's dark out there, Ragsy, like the sun disappeared or something." Her voice was a whisper.

The shutters rattled against the side of the house. She snuggled closer to Rags and wrapped her arms around him. "I hope your daddy gets home soon."

Something scraped the floor.

Rags stirred.

She scooted forward and squinted into the gloom. There didn't seem to be anything there.

"It's okay, boy. It's okay." The words were more for her benefit than his.

Rags leaned against her and whined. Robin hugged him, staring at the picture window, willing a speck of light to fall into the room, but all that spilled in were doubts and second thoughts. She should have stayed home. She should have helped her mother with the groceries. Anything would be better than this. But if she had, Rags might have died. She tightened her hold on him. She had done the right thing—she hoped. But Seth was still missing and she had no clue about where he was or why he'd abandoned Rags for four days.

When the storm broke, meager light filtered into the room. Rags jumped down from the chair and his toenails clicked across the floor. Within seconds, he scratched the front door and whined.

Was Seth really in the fields in this mess? If so, how could she find him in hundreds of acres of corn?

Rags barked and sprang hard enough against the door to make it thud in its frame. He turned a circle, jumped up, and rested his paws on her shoulders. His soft, determined eyes stared at her. *Was he telling her he could find Seth?*

When his paws dropped to the floor, she knelt beside him. "Do you know where your daddy is, boy?"

He barked and wagged his tail.

She reached for Seth's windbreaker hanging on the coat rack by the door, but pulled back her hand when, for a second, the rack looked like someone standing in the darkened corner. She grabbed it quickly and slipped it on, rolling up the sleeves. She bent down and held Rags' face. "You've got to find Seth, boy."

The dog jerked loose and lunged for the door, scratching as if he'd claw right through. She considered finding the leash, but there was no time. She turned the doorknob and the door barely opened before Rags lunged out and leaped off the porch. She panicked, as he bulleted through the light rain and down the gravel drive. She glanced around for the crow. No sign of it. She stepped onto the porch and yelled, "Hey, Rags, wait for me!"

Grave Discovery

✳ ✳ ✳ ✳ ✳ ✳

Seth's nylon windbreaker swished against Robin's knees as she ran in the rain, her feet crunching along the uneven gravel. Hail, the size of peanuts, pelted her and everything else. Kota, her friend's grandfather, called hail *wasu*—snow seeds. It was such a soft name for something so hard and painful. Life was chock-full of contradictions.

She ran until she reached the road. No sign of Rags. To make matters worse, she had a cramp in her side from running. She leaned over and pressed it while she caught her breath. As she panted, she looked to the left. Nothing but blacktop, tall corn, and rain drumming the wet road. At least the hail had stopped. She looked right and saw Rags' brown tail disappear around the curve. She didn't want to lose him. By sheer will, she gathered all the energy she had and took off running, splashing through puddles with each step. No matter how much it hurt, she told herself, she had to keep putting one foot in front of the other. Good Lord, she sounded like her gym teacher, Ms. Mosley. "Run through the pain, girls," she used to say. "It's mind over matter." Well, she hoped the old gasbag was right.

Breathless, she rounded the bend in the road and saw Rags up ahead running like a greyhound. *How did he keep up the pace?* Then he disappeared again. One second he was there, the next—poof—gone. She slowed to a walk, kicking water ahead of her while rain tapped her face. Her glasses were useless now. She removed them, tucked them in one of Seth's pockets, and wondered how the clouds could hold the weight of all that water and not crash to the ground.

As the rain steadily increased, water sluiced down her face. She wiped it with both hands while trying to look for Rags, but he was nowhere in sight. She called his name, looking down the rows as she walked, but saw only walls of corn. It was hopeless, and she was exhausted and soaked to the bone. Her shoes were water-logged and felt like they weighed ten pounds each. On top of it all, she had failed to find Seth.

Rags suddenly sprang from between two rows where the road curved east. He barked, running around in circles, and darted back into the field.

"Gotcha, you stinker," she said as she ran with her eyes glued to the spot.

When she reached the turn into the field, she stopped, stunned by what she saw. Laying before her was a wide swath of crushed cornstalks that stretched thirty feet into the field and then curved left.

Her cheeks puffed in and out. *What's going on? First the flower bed, now this.* She pushed the fear from her mind and jogged into the sloppy field, being careful not to trip on flattened stalks of corn covering the ground.

The wind whistled like air rushing through a tunnel and the deeper she went into the field, the louder the cornhusks rustled. She felt more alone than ever. *Where was Rags?* The husks rustled again. One brushed the back of her neck. She shuddered. Her skin felt like spiders were tap-dancing on it.

Overhead, slate-colored clouds rumbled and tumbled into one another, shaking out enough rain to fill a lake. Underfoot, the clay-based soil turned to soup, making her sneakers slimy and orange.

She unrolled the jacket sleeves to cover her cold fingers and heard something. *A voice? Seth's?* She cupped her hands to call out, then hesitated. *What if it wasn't him? Maybe a stranger. Maybe someone who hurt Seth. And where was Rags?* She stepped back. *What was she doing out here by herself?*

She heard it again. It was a voice, but not Seth's. And whoever it was, was moving through the cornstalks and getting closer. She back-pedaled into a stalk and cracked it off at the base. She regained her balance and was about to run when a large stone plopped into the mud at her feet. Her heart felt as if it was pounding in her head. Then, to her horror, the stalks began to part. She snatched up the stone and drew back her hand. She closed her eyes and screamed, hurling the rock with all her might.

Someone yelled, "Robin!"

Her eyes popped open as she regained her balance. In front of her was a very wet version of her friend, Alex Sanders. The rain made his hair appear to be painted onto his head. Water ran down his face and trickled off his nose. He stood there, holding the stone.

"Robin, you could have killed me."

"Alex! I didn't know who or what you were—especially when *that* came at me." She pointed to the stone.

"*That*, as you call it, is an Indian grinding stone and it's several hundred years old. Besides, I didn't know who or what *you* were. I figured if I threw the stone an animal would run or a person would say something—a *normal* person anyway."

"I was too busy being scared out of my wits, you jerk. Besides," she stepped to the next row and looked both ways, "I'm trying to find Seth."

"Out here? In this?" He shook mud from his boots.

"He's missing, Alex. And now Rags is missing, too. He was leading me to him, but I lost him—thanks to you." She called for Rags as thunder rumbled in the belly of the clouds.

Alex pressed his hand on his forehead.

"What's the matter?"

"Just, uh, weird stuff." He exhaled through pursed lips. "You're not going to believe this Robin, but hear me out."

She stuffed her hands in the jacket pockets. "Okay, but make it snappy because Rags and Seth are out here somewhere and I've got to find them."

"I was heading out of the cornfield when I—" he hesitated and looked out over the stalks, "when this, this, this big crow landed in front of me."

"Crow?" Her throat went dry.

"Yeah. At least I thought it was a crow—at first."

She squinted.

"Just listen. I tried to shoo it away, but instead of going, it waddled towards me. Then it disappeared. Just like that. And a pirate appeared. A big, mean-looking guy with all the gear—a hat, clothes and sword, standing right in front of me and blocking my path."

She blinked. "A pirate? Was his ship parked nearby?"

"Very funny. This is serious, Robin. This guy had black hair and a beard and these dark, evil-looking eyes. And that sword was a city-block long."

"City block? In a cornfield?"

He gave her a look. She pressed her lips together and motioned him to continue.

"I no sooner shook my head than the pirate was gone and the crow was back. Then there was this flutter of feathers and the bird charged right at me. It even pecked the side of my head." He leaned forward and pointed out the spot.

"Whoa," she blew out a breath. "Weird. Either that crow has a twin or it sure gets around." She held out her hand to display the now swollen, blue vein.

"A crow did that?"

"Yep. I figured it was just spooked by the storm, but now I don't know. Did you see the article in the paper? The one about the moon with the curse?"

"You know I don't read the paper, Robin. Besides, I got out here early to see what arrowheads the rain might have uncovered. What'd it say?"

"It talked about the strange moon that was out last night. The one that's upside-down."

He raised an eyebrow.

"It only appears every quarter century or so and it has a curse—a pirate's curse," she explained about the article.

"What's going on, Alex? First the moon and now the crow and pirate. I could see the crow attacking one of us. Two is pretty improbable, but still possible."

"Cut the brainy stuff. I get enough of that at school."

"I was just thinking that with the moon, the crow, and the pirate—"

"I don't know, Robin. I couldn't swear—"

"It's got to have something to do with the curse, Alex. And on top of everything, we're missing Seth *and* Rags."

31

He shrugged. "What happened to Seth?"

"I don't know, but I'm really worried, Alex. I can't find him anywhere and Rags was locked inside for days."

"Come on Robin. How do you know he was locked in for days? Maybe it was hours."

She crossed her arms. "Believe me, I know. News papers hadn't been picked up, Rags was inside, and that brown, mushy stuff all over the floor wasn't new carpet."

He grimaced. "You should have called me or Grandpa."

She propped a hand on one hip, "Kota maybe, but not you. Just because you're part Lakota doesn't mean you can track an eighteen-wheeler across a wet lawn. Besides, I was trying to call your grandpa when the phone went dead."

"And there was no sign of Seth, anywhere?"

"All I know is there were four newspapers on Seth's porch. Four, Alex." She held up her fingers. "We've got to find him." She called for Rags again.

"Where did you lose him?"

"On this path. I thought he was leading me to Seth, but he moved so fast I couldn't keep up."

He grinned.

"No jokes about my athletic ability. Not now."

He flicked her shoulder with the back of his hand. "Come on, Robster. We'll find him."

Robin shook her head. "It's hopeless. There's hundreds of acres and if the rain keeps up we'll have to build an ark."

Tell-Tale Scar

✳ ✳ ✳ ✳ ✳ ✳

Robin trembled as she stared at the gray, bloated hand sticking through the mud. She wanted to look away, but was too dazed till the sound of Rags tugging at the sleeve snapped her out of it. She grabbed his collar and pulled him back, but her eyes remained on the hand. It was distorted and discolored and more terrible than any special effects she had seen in horror movies. Yet, something niggled at the back of her brain. Something familiar. Then it hit her like a bullet train. *The scar! It was Seth's scar.* She felt lightheaded and began falling backwards, dragging Rags, breaking cornstalks and splattering mud till she toppled to the ground. Rags yelped, falling with her.

Alex came out of his daze, and covering his nose, splashed backwards in the muck.

Robin and Rags scrambled to their feet and sloshed after him. They got five or six feet, when she bent over and tossed her scrambled breakfast into the mud. She wiped her

35

mouth, and pulled soggy tendrils off her face. Rags sniffed at the muddy mess. She quickly pushed him away. Thoughts of Seth swarmed in her head—him fixing her bike, carving a pumpkin that looked like her, having talks over cocoa, and always, always listening to her. The reality of his death swept over her like a tsunami. She dropped to her knees and sobbed.

When she wound down, she noticed Rags was gone. She found him lying on the dirt where Seth was buried. She took him by the collar and pulled him out to the road where a pale, stunned Alex stared into the distance.

"Gotta get Grandpa, Robin. He'll know what to do."

"We have to call the police first."

"Grandpa and Seth were best friends since before I was born. Grandpa needs to know before anybody."

Rags tugged toward the cornfield. "Okay, but we've got to get Rags out of here, Alex. He's about to drag me through the field to get to Seth."

"I'll take him." Alex took off his belt and looped it through the dog's collar. "Now let's get going."

They trotted down the road, wiping tears and rain from their faces. At the first bend, they saw a vehicle approach. Robin stood in the road waving her arms to flag it down.

"Do you recognize the car?" Alex asked, squinting to see in the rain.

"Probably someone leaving work at the port," Robin

said, waving her arms till the car slowed. She added, "Seth's dead. And he didn't bury himself, so the sooner we get help the better."

In the diminishing rain, they watched the driver of the rusty, blue sedan hit the brakes and stop a foot from Robin. The windshield wipers thumped back and forth as she walked to the driver's side. The window lowered, letting music spill out. Something old—maybe from the eighties.

The driver looked from her to Alex. "What are you two doing in the middle of the road, and what do you want?"

Robin looked inside and didn't like what she saw. The man had dark, baggy eyes, a cigarette pressed between crooked yellow teeth, and thin hair that stuck out all over. Her eyes went from his face to his clothes, which were covered in mud. Across the backseat lay a shovel.

Robin straightened and with wide eyes looked at Alex over the roof of the car. She pretended to tuck her hair behind her ears, but was actually gesturing with her fingers for him to look into the backseat.

Alex scrunched up his face.

"I asked once," the man said, putting the car into gear, "ain't gonna ask again."

She quickly put her hand on the window's edge. "I, uh," she stammered, "noticed you have a shovel in the back."

It was loud enough for Alex to hear. He pulled Rags towards the back of the car and peered through the window.

"So what?" the man said. "Ain't no law against it."

"We, uh, found something in the cornfield and need a shovel," Robin said.

Alex shook his head real hard and ran his index finger across his throat for her to cut it off—right then.

"Well, ya ain't getting this one. I just dug out a heifer that was belly deep in mud and now I gotta go mend a fence that got washed out."

"Oh," she said. "Well, would you happen to have a cell phone we could use? It's a really big emergency."

His eyes narrowed. In the passenger's side mirror, he stole a glance at Alex looking into the car. "You kids ain't ripping me off." He stomped the gas and headed down the road.

They watched the car grow smaller as it sped away.

"Jerk!" she said.

"You shoulda told him we have to call the police."

"No kidding, Einstein. I see that now."

"Geez," he said, tugging at Rags, "I'll handle the next one—if there is one. I can't believe you carried on a conversation when you saw how creepy he looked."

"We're desperate, Alex, in case you haven't noticed."

"But he could have been the one who killed Seth."

She watched the bumper of the car disappear around the bend. "That's what I thought till he mentioned the cow. Could be anybody."

"Mentioning a cow means he's not a killer?" He shook

his head as he hurried Rags along. "You'd be great on a jury."

When they reached Alex's white frame house, they led Rags into the kitchen where Alex's mother was peeling potatoes at the sink. She turned, saw they were covered in mud, and held up her hand. "Stop right there you two—uh, three. Especially you three."

"Forget it, Mom. This can't wait. We have to call the cops right now—"

Robin interrupted, "Seth's dead." The words seemed to echo off the powder blue walls. *Seth's Dead. Was it possible?*

The potato peeler clinked onto the speckled countertop. "Dead? W—what happened?"

They told her what they knew and Mrs. Sanders made two calls: one to the sheriff, and the hardest one of all, to Kota.

Robin noticed Mrs. Sanders' hands shook, which seemed odd considering she was a nurse and should be used to all kinds of emergencies. But this one was personal—real personal.

By the time Alex and Robin changed into dry clothes, Kota stood in the doorway. He was a mountain of a man who stood six feet, four inches tall and had a barrel chest. His face was noble-looking with high cheekbones, dark eyes, and a nose that revealed his Indian heritage. His silver hair was tied in a small ponytail by a thin strip of leather. Hanging at his waist was the twelve-inch knife he always carried.

No one spoke. Their expressions and the pain in their eyes said it all.

A few moments later, Robin ran across the kitchen and threw her arms around him.

"*Šišóka*," Kota said as he hugged her.

"I had to drag Ragsy away from him," Robin said.

Rags pressed against Kota's legs. "He's a good dog. He will lead me to Seth. We'll need cord for a leash."

"I'll go with you, Grandpa," Alex said.

"No, *Mitakoja*—my grandson. You stay."

Alex found some cord and tied it onto Rags' collar as a siren sounded, wailing louder and louder till tires screeched in the street. Kota walked outside with Rags as the sheriff reached the steps.

"Hey, Kota. Ain't that Dyer's dog?"

Kota nodded. "He will find Seth."

The sheriff harrumphed while he adjusted his gun belt beneath his sagging stomach. "In case you haven't noticed, Kota, that ain't no bloodhound. Guy like you should know the difference." He spat a stream of tobacco out the side of his mouth. "It's just a stray that took up with Dyer a few years back. The kids found his body. They'll show me where it is."

"They've been through enough, Sheriff. The dog can lead us."

Alex opened the screen door. "Sheriff Woodward used to say Grandpa could track better than any dog. Said he tracked with his head. He's psychic, you know, has a sixth sense."

The sheriff took a deep breath, making his stomach seem to suck into his chest. "That was the old sheriff, son, and the old days. These are modern times now, and *this* sheriff don't waste time or use civilians."

Alex looked towards his grandfather. "Take the S-curve on Utica, Grandpa. When you see the corn smashed down you'll find him thirty feet back."

"Son," the sheriff said, burping his hat on his head like a Tupperware lid, "that's enough. There's too much corn and mud to be slopping around out there all day. Now get your shoes on and get in the back of the patrol car."

While the sheriff waited inside for Alex to get his shoes, Kota loaded Rags into the cab of his old black Dodge pick-up and headed for Pike Road.

"I'll go with you, Alex," Robin said, adjusting her glasses on the bridge of her nose. She glanced at the sheriff. "If Sheriff Newby doesn't object."

The sheriff stopped mid-chew. "Object? Just what this town needs—another lawyer."

A Killer in Bridgeport
✳ ✳ ✳ ✳ ✳ ✳

Thirteen-year-old Marc Corby saw his younger sister, Cimber, grab her gerbil and hurry to the window as a siren wailed onto the street and stopped.

She pressed the gerbil's nose to the window and looked across the street towards the Sanders' house. "Wow! Look, Mr. Whiskers!"

Marc peered over the *Boxing World* magazine with his hero, Mohammed Ali, on the cover. His relatives had told him he was the spitting image of the champion when he was a very young fighter.

"What is it?"

"Nothing you'd be interested in because you think you know ev-v-verything."

He tossed the magazine on the ottoman and walked to the window.

"I know your brain's about the size of that rat's. Now move over." When she didn't budge, he leaned forward for

42

a better look, sandwiching her against the window. Being one of the tallest kids at school had its advantages.

"It's the police!" he said. "At Alex's!"

With her face pressed against the window, she said, "Back off, you jerk! You're smashing me."

He ignored her and leaned closer.

Through squashed lips, Cimber mumbled, "Mom! Dad! Marc's hurting me!"

He bolted for the door. He jumped off the porch and nearly collided with a large blackbird swooping around the house. He ducked, lost his balance, and went down on one knee. When he looked up, the bird was gone. He heard his sister laugh, but didn't stop to retaliate because a second police car screeched to a halt.

He sprinted across the road with images of the day Alex's father died whirling in his head. He and Alex had come home from school and found Sheriff Woodward's car parked exactly where Sheriff Newby's was now. Alex's grandfather met them at the door, took Alex inside, and told him about his dad. It was a day he'd never forget. The thought of it made his stomach roll.

He reached Alex's yard as the sheriff ordered Robin and Alex into the squad car.

Marc looked at Alex and Robin and said, "You okay?"

"Son, run along home." He waved him away like a pesky fly. "We've got police business here."

Alex whispered, "S'okay. Call ya later."

Marc stepped back and watched the tan and brown police car make a U-turn and speed off with the deputy's car following.

Marc sat on the porch steps where Mrs. Sanders joined him.

"What's going on?" Marc asked. "Are they in some kind of trouble?"

"No, honey. They're helping the sheriff."

"Helping?" He shook his head. "That didn't look like Alex's helping face."

"I guess you'll be hearing this soon anyway." She folded her hands in her lap, cleared her throat, and explained everything.

"Seth? Murdered?" Marc said, staring past the end of the street to the sea of corn. "Then that means—there's a killer loose in Bridgeport."

The Body Detective
✳ ✳ ✳ ✳ ✳ ✳

When Kota opened the truck door, Rags leaped off the seat and raced through the cornfield with the cord trailing along the ground. Kota followed at a brisk pace, crunching cornhusks and stalks till he found the dog digging where the swollen, discolored hand and forearm protruded through the mud. His eyes settled on the scar. There was no doubt about it. It was Seth, the first friend he made after leaving the reservation in the western plains and coming to southern Indiana for work at the munitions plant.

Kota knelt, raised his arms toward heaven, and wailed, "*Hunhunhe*," expressing his sorrow.

As the sheriff, Alex, and Robin got out of the car, a sound pierced the air. Birds took flight in a flutter of confusion and panic. Everyone hurried into the field. Behind them a Channel 3 news van pulled onto the shoulder of the road.

When they reached Kota, they were awestruck. He was

on his knees, his arms stretched high and wide and his back arched with his face to the sky.

He wailed, *"Hunhunhe, hunhunhe, hunhunhe."* The haunting cry filled the air around them. Robin started to go to him, but Alex caught her by the arm and shook his head.

The sheriff was trying to collect his thoughts when he noticed the reporters snapping pictures of Kota. "What the— is somebody selling tickets? Grady," he yelled to the deputy, "get these people out of here. This is a crime scene, not a county fair."

Kota dropped his arms and stood. Robin wiped her nose, ducked around the sheriff and hugged Kota. "It's him, isn't it?"

"I'm afraid so," Kota said.

"I could tell by the scar," she said. "See how it sort of looks like a stretched 'W'? I asked him about it when he fixed my bicycle chain one day on Pike Road. He said it happened when his arm got caught in some farm equipment." She slipped her fingers under her glasses and wiped tears. "He was so nice. I knew something was wrong when I went to his house and found Rags all alone and Seth missing."

"Missing?" the sheriff said.

"Yes sir." She explained what happened.

"I was going to check on him today," Kota said, lifting the swollen arm with a stick to look at the underside. "I hadn't heard from him for a few days."

"Don't fool with nothing there, Kota," Sheriff Newby barked. "Dang, you're no better'n a kid."

"He wasn't killed here," Kota said, ignoring him.

The sheriff glared at him.

"He was killed somewhere else and brought here."

The deputy slid his hat back. "How do you know that?"

"Just know," Kota said.

The deputy lifted his hat and scratched his head.

"Grandpa knows everything. Ol' Sheriff Woodward used to get him to track criminals. Said he could track better than any hound dog."

"No, *Mitakoja*," Kota said. "Boasting diminishes good work. Be humble. It enhances other virtues. And a humble person rarely stumbles because they look down at the Earth and see the path ahead. Crazy Horse, great leader of the Oglala Lakota, was respected, not for his super-human acts but for being a humble man in the wake of them."

Cornstalks rustled. In the distance, a tugboat blew its whistle.

"If I remember my history correctly there, chief," the sheriff said, adjusting his gun belt, "ol' Crazy Horse didn't fare too well with the U.S. Cavalry."

"He surrendered. But at that time his people were mostly women and children and he did not want them slaughtered."

The sheriff spat tobacco on the ground between them.

Kota ignored it. "Robin's right about the scar. This is

Seth. I was with him the day he caught his sleeve in the gears of the combine. Got stitched up at Kirk Memorial. You can check their records."

"Why would someone kill Seth?" Robin said.

"I don't know, but the sheriff will find out," Kota said.

Sheriff Newby spat his whole wad of tobacco and it thunked into the mud. He pressed the redial button on his phone. "Got a possible I.D. on that corpse. Might be Seth Dyer. Repeat, could be ol' man Dyer, won't know for sure till the medical examiner digs him up."

He turned to the deputy. "Get over to the Dyer house and see what you can find. And while you're at it, call the animal shelter to take that mutt."

"No," Robin protested. "Rags can't go to an animal shelter. I'll take him."

"Robin," Alex whispered under his breath, "you know how your stepdad feels about pets."

Her heart seemed to slide to the ground.

Kota squeezed her shoulder. "It's okay, Robin. I will take him."

The sheriff nodded. "Whatever—as long as he's not running the streets."

Sirens sounded. Car doors slammed. In no time, a dozen workers trampled the cornfield. Among them were two men and a woman with medical examiner's insignias on their shirts. One began snapping pictures of the crime scene while policemen cordoned off the area and fanned out to search for evidence.

A woman, whose badge read, *Dr. Abbey Jackson, Medical Examiner* pushed her way through and examined the arm. She had a friendly, but disinterested, round face, frosted hair, and wore wire-rimmed glasses. She reminded Alex of his third grade teacher.

She nodded to the sheriff and smiled at Kota. "You're helping on this one?"

"Not anymore, Abbey."

Her smile faded. "Sorry to hear that. That intuition of yours comes in handy."

"My grandson, Alex," he touched Alex's shoulder, "and his friend Robin found the body."

She shook Alex's hand. "Guess you take after your grandfather."

Alex's face flushed. "Someday, I hope. It was Robin who figured out it was Mr. Dyer."

"Aren't you two quite the pair of detectives. And just how did you make the I.D.?"

Robin pointed to the arm, adjusted her glasses, and explained about the scar.

"Close attention to detail. You'd make a good detective, young lady."

"I'm going to be a doctor," Robin proffered. "Kind of a detective—a body detective, or maybe a disease detective."

49

Dr. Jackson chuckled. "You're right. Maybe someday you'll come work with me. Let me know if you want a tour of the medical examiner's office." She looked at Alex. "You're welcome to come, too."

"Count me out," Alex said. "I've seen enough."

The sheriff cleared his throat. "You guys through gabbing?"

Dr. Abbey Jackson snapped on some rubber gloves. "Body's been moved," she said.

Everyone looked at Kota who looked down at the pitiful grave.

She turned to one of her assistants. "Got all the pictures?"

He nodded.

"Then let's get started. Definitely moved, Sheriff. Livor mortis—sometimes called Postmortem Lividity. Blood's pooled on the front of the arm and hand—see the discoloration on the front? But he's lying on his back. When a person dies, gravity causes the blood to settle down within the vessels—not up. So he was face down when he died and brought here to the middle of the cornfield where the killer hoped he wouldn't be found. Missing tissue is due to animal activity rather than defensive wounds because there's an absence of blood and injury reaction."

Alex and Robin had seen and heard enough and headed for the road.

Kota remained till the body was unearthed.

"We'll know more when we get him downtown, but for now I'd say the cause of death was trauma to the head." Using a ballpoint pen she pointed to a three-inch gash on the top of the skull.

"Bob, get some head shots, some extras of the crown." She examined the gash more closely. "Looks like you've got a homicide on your hands, Sheriff. He was struck and either dragged or carried to this point—hard to say with all the rain and mud. By the looks of it, whoever did this was in a big hurry. Using the general rule of thumb that one day's decomposition on the ground is equal to four days buried, I'd estimate he's been in the ground three to four days."

While the Medical Examiner completed forms, Kota knelt beside the body. "*Istima, mihunka*—sleep, my brother." He rose, his heart heavy as granite, and quietly walked away.

Alex and Robin crossed the ditch where they sat on an abandoned telephone pole near the road. She folded her arms on her knees, dropped her head on them and wept. He looked the other way. The sound of her crying was more than he could bear. He sucked in a breath and while looking ahead, tried to pat her back. Instead, he hit her on top of the head.

She raised her head and gave him a sideways glance as she wiped her nose.

"Sorry," he said. "I've never been good at this kind of thing. Just trying to make you feel better."

"Glad you explained." She forced a smile, picked up a muddy stone and flung it across the ditch. "Nothing's fair—not even for Rags who's an orphan now." She exhaled. "I love that dog, Alex. I wish I could keep him. But Stanley is such a jerk about pets. It's just not fair."

Alex wasn't sure what to say. *Yeah, the man's a real jerk and your mom sure can pick 'em.* He was glad his mother hadn't remarried. No one could replace his dad.

Kota stepped out of the cornfield and called, "*Iho,*" to get their attention.

"Was it really him, Grandpa?"

"I'm afraid so."

"I'm sure going to miss him," Robin said. "He never acted like I was in the way or anything. And he taught me so many things."

Kota patted her shoulder as he sat down beside her.

"Did you know Seth could imitate twenty-one different bird calls?" she asked.

"No way," Alex said.

"Yeah. He taught me how to do a Robin's carol."

She quickly pointed a finger in Alex's face. "Don't you ev-er tell anyone, especially Brad Skeemer, or I'd never live it down."

"You know I wouldn't do that. I can't stand that punk."

"Didn't think so, but had to make sure. It's not the kind of thing a kid can do and keep their reputation. I just did it around Seth." Her bottom lip quivered. "And sometimes by myself."

"So you remember the bird people's calls, *Šišóka?*" Kota asked.

"Sure, but why do you call them bird people?"

"The Lakota believe all creatures are connected—one family on Mother Earth," Kota said. "We just have different gifts. Some have speed. Some strength. Some have the ability to fly. We humans—two-leggeds—have the ability to reason. But we are no better, just different."

"I never thought of it that way. I do remember the Robin's carol, Kota, but I don't want to do it now."

"I didn't mean for you to. The Lakota used bird people calls to communicate when an enemy was around. It's a good thing to know. There may come a time when it will save your life."

Alex squinted at Kota, but learned long ago not to always ask for explanations. He'd been taught that things are revealed in their own time.

Kota cupped his hands.

Alex and Robin listened as he caroled two and three notes at a time, broken by pauses. Alex slumped and glanced around.

Ignoring Alex, Robin said, "That was a robin. I'm certainly not that good."

"I've done it a lot longer," Kota said. "My father taught me when I was five and I taught Alex a few calls. Right, *Mitakoja*?"

Alex cringed and answered under his breath, "Yes Grandpa."

Robin stared at him.

"Crow people copy lots of sounds," Kota said. "They can even bark like a dog."

"Crows?" Robin said. "Today—"

She spotted two men at the edge of the cornfield. They were carrying a heavy-looking stretcher with a clay-smudged body bag.

"I'm glad I didn't see all of him," Robin said. "I want to remember him the way he was. The hand was enough to give me nightmares."

"Robin, a dead person is nothing to fear. Dying is like an animal shedding its skin. When people die, they shed their bodies, but their energy—their *nagi*—spiritual self—lives on and is released to go to another place. Some call that heaven. I guess the mystery of life and death is greater than we here can ever know. And death is the only truth."

Robin considered Kota's words. "So Seth's spirit and love are still here?"

"He is with us now. So you," he touched a finger to her nose, "are never alone."

She managed a smile.

54

"Life is a journey," Kota told them. "One that can be lonely and uncertain. But *Wakan Tanka*—the Great Spirit, will always be with you." He pressed his fist to his chest. "Here in your heart. Trust him and listen to the inner voice for it will mark your true course."

Instant Celebrity
✳ ✳ ✳ ✳ ✳ ✳

Monday, when they got off the bus at school, Alex, Marc, and Robin pressed through the mass of students like salmon fighting their way upstream. They reached the locker bay and dug books from their over-stuffed lockers. They talked till the warning bell sounded, signaling five minutes till homeroom. They slammed the gray metal doors and heard a squeaky voice behind them.

"Oh my gosh, Alex! You found a body. A dead one. I saw it on the news."

There was no mistaking the voice or the tiny brain behind it. Monica "The Mouth" Johnson. Her voice could stop a bull elephant at a distance of a quarter-mile. They had listened to it since the second grade.

Reluctantly, Alex turned to face her and found her inches from his face, her tight chestnut curls accentuating her pudgy cheeks. He backed against the locker.

"Tell me about it, and don't leave out any details. And

do it fast because the tardy bell's about to ring."

Alex's head filled with excuses, but they evaporated at the sight of the goddess standing beside Monica who quickly became a blur. The mystery girl was absolutely the cutest thing he had ever seen in his life—except in the movies, of course. But this was Bridgeport, the end of the earth. She had long, very blonde hair that hung over her shoulders, and huge innocent looking, pale blue eyes fringed with long lashes. She was as tall as Alex and slender, with a denim skirt and blue cotton shirt the color of her eyes. Her lips were the pink he'd once seen in a Florida sunset—warm and beckoning. She was a vision from a magazine cover. He was vaguely aware of voices sounding far off, like a TV going in another room. A thought nagged, persistent as a gnat. *What was she doing with Monica?*

Robin eyed the girl who now had Alex under her spell. She had flawless skin, white teeth, straight, silky hair—and no glasses. She was everything Robin wasn't. Robin had the feeling something was at a door she didn't want to open. The air in the hallway turned hot. She must be standing on a quiver because it seeped into her soles and rattled up her back. She looked at Alex again. He was as still as a heron about to strike. It was sickening to watch.

"Hello?" she said, snapping fingers in his face. "Earth to Alex. Come in, please."

Marc impatiently shifted his backpack.

Robin took that as a good sign that both of them weren't body-snatched.

She studied the new girl and thought she resembled Monica with maybe some special effects that thinned and enhanced. Had the two girls been doughnuts, Monica would be plain and this girl would be chocolate iced with candy sprinkles. *Did the new girl have the same squeaky voice? Was she all pretty wrappings with nothing inside?* Robin decided to have fun, but before she could ask a question, the girl spoke.

"You really found a dead body?"

"Yeah." It was all Alex could manage as he melted into her pale eyes and listened to her angelic voice.

Robin raised her voice above the clamor of students crowding the hallway. "Monica, you haven't introduced your friend."

"Oh, yeah. This is my cousin Allison." She inverted a palm and pointed to her like she was dishing up a prize on a TV game show. "We call her Allie for short. She and her mom, Aunt Lilly, just moved here from Laguna Beach. That's in California." She turned her attention back to Alex. "Now tell us the story, Alex."

Allie smiled. Deep dimples winked at the corners of her mouth. Alex slumped. That was it. He was in love.

"Bummer!" he heard Marc say. "You moved from the beach to Southern Indiana? From beaches to being beached? "Yeah, really," she said in a soft, sweet Valley Girl voice as she chewed gum. "I thought corn came from cans till I came here."

She was cool. No. Better than cool. She was ba-a-ad, Alex thought. Related to Monica? But he'd deal with that.

Allie smiled while idly fiddling with the corner of a book. She shifted the chewing gum in her mouth and Alex saw it slide across her tongue. It was pink, like her lips.

"I miss the beach, miss my board, but mom says I'll get back there someday if I'm meant to."

As she spoke, she looked right into Alex's eyes. He couldn't think of a thing to say, but was ready to pack his bags and take her to the west coast.

Allie stopped chewing, apparently waiting for Alex to respond. When he didn't, Marc stepped in. "I'm Marc Corby, by the way, and my mute friend here is Alex Sanders."

Alex elbowed him. He could talk, but his brain had turned to mush. He raised a hand and one little word popped out. "Hi."

"And I'm Robin," she said, squeezing back in. "What grade are you in?"

"Seventh. Team B."

"But what about the body?" Monica interrupted.

"Team B!" Alex said, as if winning the lottery. "So are we." She had to be in some of his classes.

"We better get to homeroom before the bell rings," Robin urged, "which is about thirty seconds from now."

Everyone scrambled. In the midst of the confusion, Alex collided with Monica. His books fell to the floor in the stampede and he watched helplessly as they were kicked again and again by scurrying feet.

"Sorry," she said. He chased the books and when he looked up, Allie was nose to nose with him. He stared into her eyes and saw the blue Pacific. The hallway seemed to fade away. He braced his knee against the tiled floor as she stood up, turned, and hurried through the crowd. The word "thanks" formed on his lips, but it was too late. When he couldn't see her anymore, he headed for homeroom.

As he ran, his mind churned. Why couldn't I say something—clever. Something memorable like they do in the movies. Women. This was new territory. He imagined he and Allie dancing in the middle of the gym floor with all the other students enviously standing around watching. He wished he'd taken those dancing lessons his mother had been egging him about.

Alex hurried into room B108 and slid into his seat as the bell stopped ringing. Mrs. Willowby peered at him over her half-glasses and waved her ruler. "That's cutting it a little close, don't you think, Mr. Sanders?"

Channel One, the morning news program, began and the class's attention turned to the TV hanging in the upper front corner of the classroom. On the screen, Jed Howard, an eighth grader, sat at a table wearing a blue and yellow football jersey, reading a watered-down version of the national news. The camera angle changed and behind him was a banner that read "Bridgeport Headline News."

"Yesterday morning," he said, "our own Alex Sanders and Robin Beekler discovered a body in a cornfield off Pike Road."

Alex's eyes nearly popped out and he slumped in his seat. To his horror, their awful yearbook pictures flashed onto the screen. He and Robin both looked like geeks. He grimaced at the thought of Allie watching in her classroom.

Everyone started talking at once. Mrs. Willowby issued a truckload of shushes to get everyone quiet. The picture was replaced by a video of Alex and Robin standing on his front porch. His shirt was askance and his cowlick stuck out, but still, he looked pretty cool. He hoped Allie was watching after all.

The entire story was shown, including the part about Robin identifying the body. Then Jed paused while someone handed him a piece of paper, which he read:

"The sheriff's office has released the identity of the man who was found dead in the cornfield. It was Seth Dyer, a local farmer and owner of the cornfield."

Students gasped. Robin exchanged looks with Alex and Marc.

"We hope to do a follow-up story with either Alex Sanders or Robin Beekler to hear firsthand what happened." Jed leaned toward the camera and said, "How about it Alex? As a football buddy you'd do an interview for Ol' Bridgeport, wouldn't you?"

Alex's stomach flip-flopped. His fingernails dug into his arm. The screen went black. Everybody turned to look at him.

"Well, Mr. Sanders," Mrs. Willowby began, "sounds like you had an exciting weekend. I'm sure it's on your mind, so would you like to tell the class about it?"

She was a major busybody. Alex knew she would pump him for every bit of information she could. He looked around. All twenty-five faces were staring at him, waiting to hear the gory details. He looked at Robin who was in the seat in front of him. She looked down at the folder on his desk and he knew he was carrying the ball.

"There's, not, uh, not much more to tell," he said finally. "Robin was there. We found him together."

"What did the body look like?" someone asked from the back of the class. As he turned to look at them, someone on the right side fired a question.

Then two rows over someone asked, "Were you scared?" He recognized the voice without looking. It was Caroline Campbell, who had given him a rabbit in the second grade. He started to answer, but was interrupted by another.

"Were his eyes open?"

"I bet he was murdered, wasn't he?" said Jeremy Foster. Alex felt dizzy. He didn't know which question to answer or whether to try.

"That's enough," Mrs. Willowby said, slapping her ruler on her desk. "You're not giving him a chance to answer. Patience is a virtue, students. Now, one at a time, please. And raise your hands."

Marc spoke up. "Maybe he doesn't want to talk about it."

"I think that's up to him, Mr. Corby." She glared at him over the tiny glasses perched low on her nose.

Marc rolled his tongue around the inside of his cheek, calming the words.

"All we saw," Alex said, "was the hand and part of his arm. The rest was buried, so I don't know anything about his body, face, or anything else. And like you heard on the news, Robin was the one who figured out who it was. The medical examiner was pretty impressed with that."

"Maybe *she* did it!" The remark came from smart-mouth Jason, one of the Kids in Black.

Alex looked at him in disbelief.

"Think about it, man," Jason said, "like, how else would she, like, know who the guy was if he was buried?"

What seemed like a galaxy of eyes looked at Robin. She pushed her glasses higher on her nose. Jason the Mouth had tagged her. She was it. She glared at him. He wore black pants, T-shirt, and combat boots. Around his neck was a black leather spiked dog collar. It was the Gothic-dumb look. Good thing it wasn't a choke collar or she'd use it.

"Well?" he pressed.

Marc had enough. "Being smart doesn't make her a murderer, Dog-breath!"

Jason jumped out of his desk and started for him, but Mrs. Willowby slapped her ruler on her desk again and he stopped.

"Boys, that's enough!" To Marc, she said, "And there's no reason to be calling anyone names, Mr. Corby. You do that again and you'll be assigned an essay."

She addressed the class. "I guess we'll have to wait for the school interview to get the whole story."

Jason sat down and Mrs. Willowby called the roll and collected book club orders.

When the bell rang, Alex breathed a sigh of relief.

Seventh graders ate during the second lunch, and by that time Alex and Robin were exhausted from all the questions asked in the classes, in the hallways, and even in the bathrooms.

They ate pizza and tried to relax while they watched a class of eighth graders swim in the pool adjacent to the cafetorium. Alex was on his second bite when he felt a hand on his shoulder. Without looking up, he tossed the pizza on the styrofoam plate and braced for another question. Then he heard Mr. Michaels, his favorite teacher. Everyone liked Mr. Michaels, the science teacher, except of course the Kids in Black who didn't think it was cool to like anything.

"Well, I've been looking for the Three Musketeers. Are you hanging in there with all the hoopla about yesterday?"

"By a thread," Alex said.

"And how about you, Madam President?" Mr. Michaels always teased Robin about becoming the first woman President of the United States.

She set down her milk carton. "Let me just say it's been a very long morning."

"I bet it has. And yesterday must have been pretty rough for both of you."

Robin nodded.

"Yes sir," Alex said. "It was like a horror movie, with lightning and thunder thrown in." He wiped his mouth, thinking he might have pizza sauce on it.

"I'll bet. Don't forget you could talk to a counselor about it. That's what they're here for. And you can always talk to me—you know that." He looked at Marc. "Of course you've always got your buddy, there."

Marc nodded, giving a thumbs up sign as he chewed.

Mr. Michaels left to nab two kids tossing French fries. "Catch you later."

Alex picked up his pizza and took another bite while watching Mr. Michaels limp away.

"He is such a nice guy," Marc said as trays clanged in the background.

"Yeah," Robin said. "And I hate the way some of the kids make fun of his leg. Someone said he had polio."

"Yeah," said Alex. "I want to pulverize them when they do that."

"I can't imagine it," Marc said. "I'd always feel like people were staring at me."

"He's pretty cool about it though," Alex said. "Like when he talks about his height and says he's 5'8", 5'10", 5' 8", 5'10". That's funny. But I don't know if I could take walking around in front of this bunch every day."

They chewed pizza while Mr. Michaels limped from table to table, talking to kids.

"Would you like to be a teacher?" Marc said.

"No way, man," Alex said, screwing up his face. "I'd rather be hit by a bus."

"Me too," Robin said. "I plan to make money, big money, and teaching certainly wouldn't give me that."

Marc wadded his napkin and tossed it on the pizza crusts. "Yeah? Well, sometimes I kind of think that's what I might like to do someday."

Alex stared while slurping his chocolate milk up the straw. "You'd be good. You're smart and cool and you'd treat kids the way Mr. Michaels does."

"Alex is right," Robin said. "But hopefully you'll come

to your senses between now and when you get out of school."

Marc spewed milk onto his tray. "Don't hold anything back, Robin. Say just how you feel."

"It's true. You'd make a great teacher, but you know what, Marc? You'd make a great anything! So don't sell yourself short."

"If Marc has his heart set on being a teacher," Alex said, "then that's what he should be. It's not always about money, Robin."

"But it'll sure buy a ticket out of Bridgeport, won't it?"

Laughter at the next table caught their attention. A kid had two straws up his nostrils.

"See what I mean?" Robin said. "I get tired of being around people with the IQ of a turnip."

"You're just fed up because of all the teasing today," Marc said. "You don't really feel that way."

"Maybe you're right," Robin said. "Kids need somebody like you. Not like Mrs. Willowby. I've just had it with everyone bugging me today—and I didn't sleep much last night."

They waited for her to explain.

She tossed her napkin onto the tray. "I kept wondering why someone would kill Seth. And I couldn't stop thinking there was a killer still out there in the dark."

The Big Stink
✳ ✳ ✳ ✳ ✳ ✳

On the bus ride home, Alex and Robin agreed to show Marc where they found Seth, but when they arrived at Marc's house, he wasn't ready because he had to clean up his room. While Marc cleaned, Alex checked out the CD's and Robin went to Cimber's room to play with the gerbil.

As Alex popped a CD into the player, Robin yelled out, "Marc, what's the gerbil's name?"

"You mean 'the rat'?" he said, stuffing clothes in a hamper.

"Don't be a jerk," she said, nuzzling the hand-sized animal as she walked into the room.

Marc cringed. "Get that thing out of your face. You don't know where it's been."

"What's his name?"

"I hate to even say it—Mr. Whiskers," he said, stacking the loose CDs below a black and white poster of Mohammed Ali. "He's worthless. All he does is eat and poop. His cage is disgusting."

"He *is* a little poochy," she said.

"Hurry up, Marc," Alex said. "I'm getting sick watching this."

She held up the gerbil. "I wonder how long he'll live."

"Not long if he gets loose in my room again."

Robin glanced at the sheets of notebook paper, sports magazines, shoes, and socks still littering the floor. "*I'd* even get lost in here. Want a shovel?"

"Just shove it in the closet," Alex said. "That's all I do." Marc kicked a pile of clothes into the closet and heaved his shoulder against the door to close it.

"How can the rest of your house look spotless while your room looks like a dump?" she asked.

Marc's eyes narrowed and his lips formed a tight line. "If I could get a little help it wouldn't, and we might get out of here before we graduate."

"Okay! Let me put Mr. Whiskers back in his cage. By the way, his dish is empty. Where does Cimber keep the food?"

"It's always empty. The food's in a fifty-pound bag in the utility room behind the garage. Door's unlocked. And hurry up so we can finish and get out of here before my parents get home."

When they reached the cornfield, they propped their bikes along a row of cornstalks. As they walked deeper into the field, Alex told them he was worried about whether he could still hunt for arrowheads now that Seth had died.

Trying to keep up, Robin said, "Who takes over the farm?"

Alex thought about it. "I don't know. His wife died about ten years ago. He has a son, but I don't think he lives around here."

"He had a lot of land, didn't he?" Marc said.

"Hundreds of acres, mostly corn. Some planted in wheat."

"He must have been worth millions!" she said.

"Doubt it," Alex said, screwing up his face. "My grandpa was always pitching in to help him fix something. If he'd been wealthy he would have hired somebody."

"I was just working on a motive," she said, "because somebody might have wanted to get their hands on the land."

"Especially," Marc said, running ahead, then walking backwards to face them, "*especially* if this person found out there was something valuable on it—like, say gold or oil. Or maybe something we don't even know about, like some kind of rare mineral they need for the space program."

"That's it!" Robin said. "Maybe the killer's been trying to get him to sell his land and he wouldn't, so he iced him. Kaboom! Just like that!" She smacked her fist in her open hand.

Alex puckered his brow. "The land's full of Indian artifacts, but nothing to kill for."

Still caught up in the drama, she ignored him. "Then they had to dispose of the body. What better place than the middle of all this?" she stretched out her arms. "Who would dream someone could find the body here?"

Before Alex could answer, his eyes fixed on yellow crime scene tape with the words, POLICE CRIME SCENE—DO NOT CROSS. It had been looped in and out of the cornstalk perimeter. Beyond the tape, a half acre of tall corn had been trampled to the ground, making it look like a battlefield of fallen soldiers.

"They've ruined everything!" Alex's face turned as red as his shirt. He ducked under the tape and carefully stepped between the flattened stalks. "Just look at it."

"It's okay, man," Marc said. "There's plenty more out there."

"No, you don't understand," he said. "It's not just the corn, although that's bad enough. This is the best Indian artifact site in the entire southern Indiana region. There are all kinds of things in the soil. Arrowheads, spearheads, pottery, *history*. And it's probably all crushed. Look at it." He blew out a breath, snagged a corncob from the ground, and flung it into the distance.

While Alex paced, Robin and Marc cleared an area on the ground and sifted the dirt for clues.

When he calmed down, Alex said, "This is all because of the dream."

"Dream?" Robin said, looking up. "So much has happened, I'd forgotten about it. You kept having it over and over, right?"

"Three nights in a row—before all this happened. Each time I was here in the cornfield. I was running and I tripped over what I thought was a branch, but when I looked back, I saw this hand sticking out of the ground." He demonstrated with his hand.

"Alex," Robin said, "you had a dream that later came true? That's like psychic, you know, like your grandpa."

"I'm not psychic. I just have lots of dreams—every night."

"That come true?" she said, grabbing another handful of dirt and letting it sift through her fingers.

"It's the dream catcher," he said.

"The one your grandpa made you?" Marc asked.

"Yeah. He hung it by my bed and in front of the window overlooking the cornfield."

"But don't you see?" Robin said. "It's like a prophecy."

"Of course I see. Why do you think I'm bringing it up now? I mean the dreams were in color and were as real as the three of us right here in this cornfield. And they were really scary. I woke up screaming each time I saw that hand sticking up."

"I think it's more complicated than that. We need to figure this out. This calls for a 'Three Musketeers Night.'"

"She's right," Marc said. "This is a little too weird. And by the way, I think we've outgrown the Three Musketeer's gig. We need to call it something else. The Big Pow Wow or something."

"You mean, kind of like a G-8 Summit," Robin said, adjusting her glasses.

Marc and Alex scrunched up their faces as though she were talking a foreign language.

"It's a conference of world leaders—"

Alex cut her off. He wondered how much he really wanted to know about anything, but said, "Okay. This Friday, at my house?"

They nodded, hit fists, and stacked them.

"Mom's got to work at the hospital, but I'll ask Grandpa to be there."

"Settled," Marc said.

Robin stooped, pinched soil between her fingers. "I wonder what the geological surveys show for this area."

Marc looked at Alex and rolled his eyes.

She watched the soil drift through her fingers. "It would take some time, and research, but it's worth looking into." She scooped another handful of dirt from beside a flattened stalk. She squeezed it and discovered a broken key chain.

"What's that?" Marc asked.

"Don't know." She brushed it and blue fur appeared.

"It's a lucky rabbit's foot."

"Seth's?" Marc said.

"Doubt it," she said. "He wasn't the kind of guy to carry a rabbit's foot around."

"Then maybe it belongs to the killer," Alex said, taking the foot to examine it. "And maybe his luck will run out."

Marc's eyes went past Alex to a large hole in the ground. "Is that it? Where Seth was buried?"

Alex nodded.

They no sooner reached the spot than a man's voice bellowed behind them. "What are you kids doing here?"

Robin jumped and turned around so fast, her ponytail smacked Alex in the face. He batted away the hair, and saw Sheriff Newby and Deputy Grady approaching.

"Oh great," Alex groaned. "This guy hates kids."

The sheriff looked peeved. "This is a crime scene," he said, walking up to Alex. "No one's allowed here unless they're on police business, which, of course, you kids ain't. So run along and play." He turned to his deputy. "Get more of that tape out here, Grady. And on the double."

"We're not playing, Sheriff Newby," Alex said. "Mr. Dyer said I could come here anytime."

The sheriff shoved his hat back on his head and leaned into Alex's face. Alex could smell coffee and tobacco on his breath.

"Well, Seth Dyer isn't around anymore, is he? So scat."

"We're working on the case," Robin said.

Alex nearly choked.

Robin glared at him.

"You're *what*?" The sheriff said, his fists on his hips. "We don't have time for foolishness. And we certainly don't want kids messing around the crime scene. Now leave before I haul your sorry butts down to the station for interfering with police business!"

Robin snatched the foot from Alex's hand and held it up. "Well, here's a little something you missed."

"Where'd you get that?"

"Over there," she pointed to the edge of the trampled corn. "It was in a dried clod of clay." She crossed her arms. "Guess somebody didn't do their job working the scene."

"We combed this whole area," Grady said, "so you kids probably just dropped it here."

"So *you're* responsible for all this?" Alex said, his face reddening. "Look at all the corn you guys trampled—not to mention all the Indian artifacts."

"Now you listen to me, son, and listen real good 'cause this is the last time I'm going to say this. Get out of here right now or I'm gonna haul your butts downtown and make your parents come to get you at the jail. Now scat!"

The cork on Alex's anger was close to blowing. This was their concern as much as the sheriff's. He didn't care what the man said. Heck, let him take them to jail. *That* would make the news—and get nationwide attention. But a voice inside him said, *Leave it. Let it go!*

"I don't want to see you around here again," the sheriff said. "Is that clear?"

Alex nodded, kicked a clod of dirt, and walked away.

Out of earshot, Marc said, "Talk about a jerk!"

"Yeah," Robin added. "He's going to wish he hadn't been so obnoxious when we solve this case."

"*We?*" Alex's eyes widened.

"Yeah," Robin said. "We're going to solve this thing if I have to stay up every night doing research for the rest of my life." She smacked a fist into her palm. "I'll do as much as I can by Friday night. We'll show him. We'll—" She paused, pushed her sliding glasses back in place, and sniffed. "What's that horrible smell?"

"Gag a maggot!" Marc pulled his jersey over his nose.

"It ain't perfume," Robin gasped.

"I smelled that yesterday," Alex said. "What is it?"

"Some kind of chemical," she said. "I've smelled it before, but can't place it." She turned, sniffing in different directions, causing her eyes to water. "Where's it coming from?"

"Don't know," Alex said, "but yesterday morning I smelled it near the road." He pointed. I didn't see any containers or anything, but I'll tell you this, Seth never used pesticides. He was an organic farmer. He used B.T. instead."

"What's that?" Marc said.

"Bacillus Thuringiensis," Robin said. "People use it in their garden."

Marc shook his head. "Whatever." He sniffed, and wiped his eyes. "Might be coming from the Port. Maybe the wind's blowing from that direction."

"Maybe, but whatever it is," she said, "it's putrid. Let's get out of here before we get sick."

When they retrieved their bikes, Robin told them good-bye and headed for her house. After she left, Alex and Marc laughed about her solving the case till they rode around the curve and smelled the odor again.

"Smells like liquid plastic," Alex said.

"The wind's definitely carrying it this way," Marc said. "It even seems like it's following us."

Alex pedaled harder. "First the murder, now this stink. What's happening to Bridgeport? It's been such a great town."

Marc stopped pedaling. "Great?"

"Well, it's a small town anyway. They're supposed to be safe, right?"

They rode into a bend where trees bordered the ditch and cast shadows that darkened the curve. Overhead, a barn owl screeched. Marc looked at Alex and said, "I don't know how safe this town is anymore. Let's step on it, so we won't have to find out." They stood and pedaled as fast as they could through the long shadows.

77

Pythagoras

✳ ✳ ✳ ✳ ✳ ✳

On Tuesday Robin had an early dental appointment and was supposed to arrive at school by second period. Alex and Marc, however, never saw her. When she hadn't turned up by lunchtime, they worried whether she should have ridden home alone from the cornfield the day before. Especially considering what had happened to Seth.

When they approached their fifth period math class, Alex stopped abruptly and pointed toward the doorway.

"Oh man," Marc said as he spotted Robin, "I *hate* it when she wears her hair down. It looks like a burning bush growing out of her shoulders. She needs to tie it back or whack it off."

When they entered the classroom, Robin saw Alex staring incredulously at her hair. She stammered in exasperation. "I'm, well, I'm lucky to be here at all. Honestly, I don't understand how parents think sometimes. Especially my stepdad. I mean, they're supposed to be the adults, right?"

Marc glanced at the other students squeezing by. He knew they were listening to her tirade, but Robin was apparently too wound up to stop.

"I must have told him a million times, 'I have to get to school.' But he kept saying, 'We have plenty of time.' That was before a stop at the gas station, another one at the drug store, one at the cleaners, and, would you believe a stop at a phone booth? I was fit to be tied. I don't understand why he couldn't use his cell phone. I'll never let him take me to an appointment again."

Alex looked to Marc as they walked to their desks, but kept his mouth shut.

Robin dug pencils out of her book bag and checked the points. "Hold on," she said, then headed for the pencil sharpener by the door.

She had to wait while Monica sharpened four pencils, stopping to blow the dust off each one. Robin folded her arms in disgust and tapped her foot. When Monica finished, Robin gripped one pencil between her teeth and stuck the other in the sharpener. As she ground away, Brad Skeemer, her nemesis since the third grade, stepped through the door and stared at her hair. A smirk on his face, he grabbed a handful of it and gave a quick yank. She shrieked, dropping her pencil to the floor and breaking the point. She rubbed the back of her head as she whirled around and faced red strands dangling from Brad's fingers.

He smiled as he opened his hand, and watched the hairs drift to the floor.

Marc leaned toward Alex. "He's at it again."

"B-r-r-rat!" Robin said, perching her fists on her hips and feeling her cheeks redden.

"That's *Mr.* Brad to you, bird brain." He shoved her shoulder with the heel of his hand as he sneered down at her.

Marc quickly stepped between them, bumping Brad with his chest. "I'd hate for Robin to make you cry again, Brat. So, back off."

"That happened in the third grade—and it was a lucky punch. She didn't cut my lip. That happened when I fell on the bench."

Marc glared down at him, their faces nearly touching.

"Boys!" Ms. Newton yelled. "You're not here to smooch—you're here to learn math. Now go to your seats and park it."

Brad and Marc glared at one another the entire time they walked to their desks.

"Thanks," Robin whispered to Marc as he sat down. She looked at her pencils in disgust. One was still unsharpened and the sharpened one now had no point at all. She slumped into her seat. She didn't like feeling unprepared for class. School was one of the most important things in her life. It was the only thing she excelled at.

Alex saw her looking at the pencils. "I've got an extra

one." He fished it out of his book bag.

While Ms. Newton checked attendance, Robin whispered to Alex and Marc that the police had announced how Seth died.

"How?" Alex said.

Robin ducked down behind the person in front of her to keep from being seen by Ms. Newton. "Hit in the head with a tire iron."

"Ouch!" Marc said. "Did they say who did it?"

"Nope. That was all."

Ms. Newton tapped her desk. "Before we start checking homework, let's talk about the brain teaser you had for extra credit. Do you remember the question? What is *pi*? You learned its numerical approximation of 3.14 or 22 / 7, but what is it and where did it come from?"

In the ensuing silence everyone tried to look invisible. Ms. Newton's bonus questions were always tough and often involved research. Robin looked around, then raised her hand.

Alex stared at her back and figured her glasses were probably coasting down her nose as she waited. Her red hair and cobalt blue eyes made her face seem like a red, white, and blue bull's-eye—with two centers. She was the bookworm and the brain in their group—major brain. She would become a doctor one day, if for no other purpose than to remove Brad Skeemer's tongue. Ms. Newton called on her.

From across the aisle, Marc watched Robin push her

glasses up. He had seen her do that for years and figured the maneuver also pressed her brain into gear.

"Pi," Robin said, "was discovered by ancient Greeks. It's the ratio between the circumference and the diameter of a circle."

"Very good." Ms. Newton sat on the stool in the front. "Class, this is the first time a student has ever answered that bonus question, and you did it so succinctly, Robin. You get five bonus points, young lady, because you really had to do some digging to get that one."

"Like she needs them," someone blurted out.

"I guess we all know that Robin doesn't need the points, but points aren't always what's important," Ms. Newton told them. "Sometimes it's the challenge and the quest for knowledge. And, by the way, that ratio is a very special one. Let me draw you a diagram."

As Ms. Newton stepped to the chalkboard, Alex thought about how much the teacher seemed to love math. She lived for it. Even named her dog Pythagoras, after an ancient Greek mathematician. She called him Thag for short. So she was possessed, but still pretty cool—for a teacher anyway.

Drawing a circle with a line across the center Ms. Newton said, "You see, the Greeks had secret societies, kind of like clubs where they would meet to tinker with math. And it was that tinkering that gave us some profound discoveries. Discoveries that included formulas and mathematical relationships that we still use today in math and science. And we not only use them in the classroom, but even in the space program. So they were pretty smart people, huh?"

One of the Kids in Black yawned loudly. Ms. Newton asked him to get the paper measuring tape from the supply cabinet. He ambled to the back of the room, then shuffled to the front to hand it to her. She thanked him and he returned to his seat more awake.

Ms. Newton picked up a white plastic cup from her desk. "You see, when the Greeks began playing around with circles they found that every time they measured the distance around a circular object, like this cup for instance—" She held the cup higher for everyone to see and wrapped the tape around the rim.

"By the way, what do we call the distance around the circle?" she said.

Marc raised his hand and was called on. "The circumference."

"Good, Marc. So every time they measured the circumference and then measured the distance through the center, which we call—"

"The diameter," the new girl, Allie, said. Alex's head jerked like a homing device. With all the hoopla involving Robin, he hadn't even noticed she was in the class. What a break! She wasn't only beautiful, she was smart on top of it.

"That's right, Allison. Every time they measured the circumference and divided it by the diameter they got the exact same number: 3.14. They named it pi. And that's the special ratio or relationship that's used any time you do calculations that involve a curved object. It doesn't matter whether you're working with a circle, a cylinder, or even a slice of pizza, you have to use pi to do your calculations."

Robin was in heaven. To her, Ms. Newton was the Goddess of Mathematics and she worshiped at her feet. She was also known as Number Woman—a name she gave herself when she dressed in a mask and red cape with numbers all over it. She could make numbers come to life and she was doing it right then. Robin stared into space. She was somewhere in ancient Greece in a small, candlelit room scribbling computations of numbers and formulas on some kind of parchment paper.

Yes, she thought, she would have been one of them. Heck, she *was* one of them. If only she could start her own secret math society. She looked around the classroom for potential recruits. When she looked at Marc, then Alex and the others, her enthusiasm waned. Sports demons had taken over their brains, and there was no hope, except for—the new girl. She made a mental note to talk to her, and to Ms. Newton.

While Robin planned, Jed tapped at the classroom door and asked to speak to Alex. Seeing his Media Class badge, Ms. Newton let Alex go into the hallway to talk. By the time they finished their conversation, Alex had reluctantly agreed to do the interview for the school news TV program. When he returned to his desk he found Monica grading his homework with a thick red marker while students called out answers.

When Alex saw how his paper looked like a bloody battlefield, he snatched it from her, and whispered, "What's the matter, you couldn't find neon?"

"I was just trying to help," she squeaked.

The smirk on her face told him otherwise. Oooh. He hated being on the same planet with her. But Allie was in the picture now and the entire equation had changed. He would have to be nice to Monica. The pizza in his stomach churned. *Was Allie really worth it?* He looked across the room at her. Without a doubt, she *was*.

With minutes left in the class period, Robin raised her hand and was called on. "Ms. Newton, the Greeks weren't the only ones who thought circles were important. Just ask Alex. He'll tell you."

Alex's eyes nearly bulged out of his head.

Robin rotated in her seat to look at him. He shrugged his shoulders as he inverted his palms. Best to play dumb.

"You know," Robin said, "the Lakota, like your grandpa taught us." She looked at him over her glasses, but he still played dumb.

"You weenie," she mumbled under her breath, and turned back to the front. "Alex's Lakota grandfather says circles are an important part of nature, too. Like, the sun and moon are circles and they also move in circular motions. And ponds ripple and make circles. Lots of things start and end at the same place, like seasons and the calendar. Indian tepees and sweat lodges were circular. His grandfather says everything flows in a circle."

"Thanks, Robin." Ms. Newton said and looked at Alex. "Your grandfather must be a very smart man."

Alex corrected his posture and sat taller in the seat.

Then to the class, Ms. Newton said, "We have a lesson coming up in which you will learn how particular numerical ratios are found throughout nature, from sunflowers to sea shells, and even in the human body." The bell rang and class was dismissed.

Alex and Marc waited for Robin in the hall so they could ask about Seth and the news broadcast. When she finally appeared, she was with Allie.

Alex nearly dropped his books. "Look who Robin's talking to. And just when I felt like I could strangle her. What a stroke of luck. If she and Allie become friends, I can see Allie all the time."

"Then you'd get sick of her," Marc predicted.

Alex ignored him as the two girls approached.

"Hi Alex," Allie said with a bright smile.

She remembered his name. "Hi Allie. How was your first day?"

"Today's my second day."

"Ohh, yeah, I knew that." He smiled sheepishly.

"It was good, but everyone's like total strangers."

"I guess moving is really tough," Alex said. This was his chance to show his sensitive side. "Especially when you have all new classes and teachers. But you can call me if you have any questions about school or Bridgeport—"

"She can ask me," Monica declared, invading their space. "She has family here, ya know? She didn't just jump off the space shuttle or nothing."

"Or *anything*," Robin said through clenched teeth.

Monica stared at her. "Whatever, birdbrain."

It was a name Robin hated and Alex knew it. As Robin glared at her, he entertained the thought of ripping Monica's forked tongue out of her head, but Allie's voice brought him back to reality.

"Thanks, Alex. I might take you up on that. And I might take you up on your offer, too, Robin."

Robin's scowl melted to a smile. She slid her glasses up with her finger and said, "Great, we'll talk about it later."

When Allie left, Alex grilled Robin. "What offer? About what?"

Robin started to explain, but the intercom came on. She waited for the Vice Principal to stop talking. To Alex, the pause seemed as long as English class.

"I hate that thing!" Alex said when it finally stopped.

"Math Club," Robin said. "Like the ancient Greeks.

She's going to help me start one."

Alex slumped.

Robin studied him. "You've fallen for her, haven't you?"

Alex just looked down the hall. He couldn't join a math club, even if it did mean being with Allie.

"Oh, I get it. It's a hormone thing, isn't it?" Robin teased.

Alex shook his head and walked away.

"Back off," Marc said, then followed him.

Robin did some fast thinking and hurried after them. "Alex, one of the things a math club does is tutor students." Marc and Alex kept moving, so she quickened her pace. "You know, like a service project. *And,*" she said, "I might arrange for a certain *someone* to help a certain someone *else* with his geometry—whether he really needs it or not."

Alex stopped. A smile spread slowly across his face while he waited for Robin to catch up. He put an arm around her shoulder and said, "You know, Robin, this geometry stuff really has me stumped."

"Oh, I thought it might," she said. She wasn't sure why, but she liked feeling his arm around her.

What Goes Around...

✳ ✳ ✳ ✳ ✳ ✳

On Wednesday, Alex did the TV interview with Jed and for a day was the big celebrity around school. He also became more infatuated with Allison DuPree, even changing his routes to classes to see her. On Thursday, with tests on his mind, he still went out of his way to see her in the hall.

Early Friday morning Robin caught up with Marc and Alex at the locker area and said, "I had Mom drive me to the public library last night and you won't believe what I found." She talked while working the combination on her locker. When she lifted the handle, the door sprang open and she screamed as a waterfall of birdseed spilled out.

Marc caught her books as they slid across the floor on a wave of seed. Alex grabbed tied-together gym shoes. All Robin could do was watch as the remaining contents of her locker clattered onto the floor. In the grainy mound around her ankles, she saw her calculator, hair brush, and a small pack of tissues.

Brad's voice sounded behind her as he and his buddies walked past, laughing. "Hey, birdbrain! You must really be hungry!"

Marc kicked a pile of birdseed in their direction causing Brad to slip on it and land on his rear. Students howled with laughter. Soon they were scooting and sliding, riding the seed as though they were on invisible skateboards.

Marc watched Brad and his friends push two sixth graders out of their way. "I'm going to nail those guys one of these days."

Robin grabbed his arm. "Don't, Marc! Don't waste your time. Besides, you'd get into trouble and be suspended from the next football game. And then everybody in school would blame me." While holding him back, she looked to Alex. "Help me talk some sense into him."

"Talk to him? I'd like to do the same thing. They're creeps and they need to be put in their place. You saw how they treated those younger kids."

"What goes around comes around," she said. "You'll see."

The guys finally relaxed while Robin looked down at the mound of seed covering her feet.

"You know, I hate to waste all this."

"You're not thinking about scooping it up, are you?"

"I've got a family of cardinals living in that maple tree outside my bedroom window. They'd love all this."

"I'm leaving," Marc said, handing her the books.

Alex laid the shoes on top of the books in her arms. "See ya," he said and followed Marc.

"Don't forget tonight," she called after them. "You won't believe what I found out this week."

Alex stopped. "What?"

She raised her chin above the pile of books and shoes. "I'm not saying. You have to wait for tonight, but I'll tell you this: it's going to be a night we'll never forget."

Alex considered her words while he watched her drop the pile into the locker and scoop birdseed into her book bag. A creepy feeling settled over him, like a spider crawling up his back. Finally, he shook it off and headed to class.

Alex was relieved when the bell rang, ending seventh period. It had been a long Friday, more like a Monday, even though they didn't have football practice. He walked as quickly as he could to B wing so he could see Allie on his way out to the bus. After all, it would be three whole days before he would see her again.

"What's the rush?" Robin said, struggling to carry her books on one hip, the book bag of seed over her shoulder, and keep up with him.

"No rush." But he sped up just the same, trying to lose Robin by the time he met up with Allie.

When Alex reached the intersection of A and B wings, he saw Allie talking to Jed Howard and stopped on a dime.

Jed. Mr. Ego. He was the news anchorperson and the quarterback on the football team. Double cool. Double threat. Alex's knees buckled.

They hadn't seemed to notice him, so he turned around, but ran right into Marc who stumbled back, stepping onto Robin's foot. Alex ducked around them.

"Hey, Bud," Marc said, then noticed the Allie and Jed duo. He turned and caught up with Alex. "I hate that guy. He's so full of himself."

"Apparently not everyone feels the same way," Alex said.

"Won't last," Robin said, trotting to keep up and still not lose the pile of books. "Allie will get wise to him real fast."

Alex hurried to the front door and hit it so hard it banged against the doorstop.

Robin caught up with him. "You should've walked right on by to show it didn't bother you."

"You know how Jed is, Robin. He'd say something smart. Then I'd have to defend myself and get the crap beat out of me in front of her." He grabbed the book bag from her shoulder and slung it over his.

"Thanks," she said, "but you're going to run into him at some point when she's around, so you better figure it out before then."

When the bus reached Robin's stop, she turned to Marc and Alex. "Seven?"

They nodded.

"I'll bring candy and junk," she said as she left the bus.

Marc looked at Alex. "She's bringing her computer games, right?"

"She usually does," Alex said, looking absently out the window. "What do you think she came up with that would make it a night we wouldn't forget?"

"Couldn't be much," Marc said, watching a sporty SUV roar past the bus.

"I don't know. Robin's pretty smart. Just look at the brainteaser she solved today. Nobody else ever has." Alex picked up his books and ambled toward the front of the bus. "Guess we'll find out tonight."

A little before seven, Marc arrived and found Alex in the den watching a sitcom. He sniffed the air and dropped his sack of nachos, cheese dip, and Tabasco popcorn onto the floor.

"Smells good in here. Your grandpa's deer stew?"

"Yeah. He left some for you on the stove."

Marc hurried to the kitchen with Rags in his wake.

"Grandpa already fed him, so don't give him any."

Marc nearly finished the bowl of stew when he noticed Rags staring intently at him. He considered the last bite of meat and potato, glanced down the hall to make sure the coast was clear, then let Rags wolf it down in one lick and a chew.

On his way back from the kitchen, Marc caught sight of Robin rolling into the drive with her bicycle loaded down with a backpack and satchel. She propped her bike by the front steps and headed for the door. He opened it to let her in and Rags scampered to meet her, sliding the last few feet on the polished oak floor. Robin dropped her backpack with a ka-plop, and petted him. While she tussled with Rags, she asked Marc to get the satchel off her bike.

"Ragsy! You're so beautiful. How've you been?" The dog licked her face and wagged its tail. "I've really missed you, fella." She pulled a couple of rawhide dog chews from her pocket. "Here's your treat."

Alex joined them and lifted the backpack as Marc returned. "This feels too heavy for computer games."

She slapped her forehead. "I forgot them."

They stared at her.

"But wait till you see what I found. It's all right here," she said, taking the backpack from him and hugging it to her chest as though it were the Holy Grail.

"All I can say is, a genie better pop out of that bag and grant wishes for computer games," Alex grumbled.

"I thought we were going to talk about Seth's murder and your dreams," Robin countered.

Marc and Alex flopped onto the couch while she hoisted the satchel onto the coffee table.

"Let's see what she's got," Marc said.

She dumped the contents, knelt down, and sorted the papers into piles. Marc and Alex slumped. Their evening had gone down the toilet.

"Now," she said, pointing a finger at Alex, "tell us everything about the dreams. And I mean *everything*! Don't leave out a single detail because it may be important."

He knew she wouldn't give up, so he gulped his Dr. Pepper and explained about the dreams. In the process, they consumed three bowls of popcorn, a large bag of chips with dip, and three candy bars. Alex waited for a response.

Marc burped and said, "We ordering pizza?"

Robin dropped her head onto the coffee table and rolled it from side to side in frustration.

Thirty minutes later, Robin took her first bite of Papa John's pepperoni pizza. It had smelled too good to pass up. As she pulled the slice from her mouth, strands of hot, melted cheese dangled from her lips. She wrapped them around her finger and nibbled. "You can't beat our hometown pizza." She broke off a piece for Rags. "By the way, did you ask your grandpa if Seth had any relatives? Other than Rags, of course."

"Yeah, I asked him today. Seth's wife and two brothers have all died. He has one son, Sonny, who lives in Madison."

She peered over her glasses. "So the son inherits Seth's property?"

"That depends on what the will says." The voice came from behind them. They turned, saw Kota in the doorway wearing jeans, a plaid shirt, and slippers. His shoulders were nearly the width of the doorway.

"If there was one," he said, heading for the easy chair. "In the state of Indiana, property goes to the next of kin unless a will states otherwise. Why do you want to know?"

"We're working on a motive for Seth's murder," she said. "*We're* going to solve it."

"We're going to *try* to solve it," Marc clarified.

"And how do you plan to do that?" Kota said, making himself comfortable.

Marc and Alex looked at one another. That part was still a mystery to them, too. They looked at Robin.

"Motive!" she said, raising her index finger in the air. "You find the motive and you find the killer—or maybe killers. There may be more than one person involved in all this, you know."

Robin waved her hand over the papers like Moses parting the Red Sea. "That's what all this is about. I've been trying to determine whether there's anything other than the land and crops that could be of value on Seth's property. That's why I got all this." She reached into the pile and extracted a large, weathered map with Kirk County written at the top in large blue letters.

Kota lowered the footrest and leaned forward to look

over her shoulder. "That's a geological survey. Where'd you get that?"

"My uncle."

"Ah. He works for the Conservation Department, doesn't he?" Kota said.

"Yes sir. I think you met him. His name is Bob. Bob Beekler."

"He's really cool, Grandpa. He organizes our field trips to the state forest."

Marc looked down at the map as he started on the bag of popcorn. "What's with the wavy lines?"

"That's the aquifer," Robin said, "the water that runs beneath the entire southern Indiana area. Now let me show you something else." She opened a folder, pulled out documents, and pointed to sections she'd highlighted.

"There's no oil or precious metals anywhere on Seth's property. So, if someone's interested in the land, that's all they're interested in because there's nothing underneath it, except the water in the northeast section."

"How about Indian artifacts?" Alex asked.

"Well, unless they're made of gold," Robin said, "I don't think anyone would kill for them. But, I checked that anyway." She pulled a manila folder from the bottom of the stack.

Kota covered the smile forming on his lips.

"Ten years ago," she said, pushing her glasses into place,

"Seth gave Indiana University permission to do test digs for Indian artifacts. They dug rectangular sections all over his property, took what they thought was important for research and covered up the holes."

Alex's eyes widened. "Why would Seth allow them to do that?"

"They were trying to learn more about our past," Kota explained. "That's why Seth agreed."

Alex crossed his arms. "Sounds like plundering to me."

"That's because you want the artifacts for yourself," Robin said. "What about the information it provides for everybody else?"

"Does that information change our lives?" Alex asked.

"Does it have to?" Kota countered.

Alex's lips pressed into a thin line. His grandfather wanted to protect Indian artifacts—he knew he did—so why was he siding with Robin? He didn't like the direction the whole evening was taking.

She continued, "The bottom line is—they didn't find anything of note."

"Which was good for Seth," Kota said, "If they had, they would have dug up the whole field and ruined his crops."

Robin nodded. "So, we're back to square one—the land. Just land and nothing more."

"Which someone could sell," Marc said. He popped a handful of the spicy popcorn into his mouth.

Robin sipped some cola, then said, "Hey, you guys, we're talking hundreds of acres of real estate. That should be worth *some* money."

"Not all that much as farmland," Kota said, "but if someone learned the land was intended for another purpose, it might be very appealing."

"Like what other purpose?" Robin asked.

"Well," he said, "if someone learned that a road was going to be built across Seth's property, or if someone wanted to build a subdivision, then the land would be worth considerably more than it would be as farmland."

She smacked the flat of her hand on the table. "That's it!"

"But how do we find out who or what it is?" Alex asked.

"That's the hard part," Kota said, "especially if it's still just a plan in someone's head."

Robin dropped her pizza slice onto the box. "That's great. We can't go around reading people's thoughts." As soon as the words were out, she looked at Alex and Marc, then they all looked at Kota.

"Now wait a minute," Kota said. "It doesn't work like that. That would be violating a person's private thoughts. I do not do that. But I will check with some of my friends on the Planning and Zoning Board to see if anything's in the works or if they've heard any rumors."

"You know, that has to be it," Robin said. "Someone wants that land because they know it will bring a lot of money. But they had to get possession before Seth found out about the plans or he would never sell to someone who would cover the land with buildings, asphalt, or cement."

"Yeah," Alex agreed. "He loved his land."

"So," Robin said, "they, or the son, murdered him. With Seth out of the picture, his son would have it all and could sell it for whatever he wanted." Robin slapped the table again, making her cola can rattle on the surface. "Case solved. Sonny Dyer did it."

Marc held up his hands. "Wait a minute. You can't forget the thing about the will. That could blow your whole theory out the window."

"But who else would he leave it to?" Alex asked.

Kota thought about it. "Seth was very concerned about the environment and some of his land was designated as a wildlife preserve. He could have left part of it to the state for the protection of wildlife."

"But would the son know that?" Robin asked.

"Maybe, maybe not," Marc said.

"I say the jury is still out on this one," Kota said. "So I'm going to take a nap. Wake me up when you're ready to go home, Robin."

He reached the door and stopped to say, "Keep in mind that the police are conducting their own 'official' investigation. So don't do anything that would interfere or be dangerous."

After he left, Robin said, "I don't know about you guys, but I wouldn't do anything dumb."

"The whole thing is dumb, if you ask me," Alex said. "We're seventh graders, for gosh sakes. We don't have any business getting involved in a murder. Especially when the killer's still on the loose."

"The way I see it," Marc said, "there's nothing else we can do. I mean, we're just kids. The police have all kinds of surveillance equipment and stuff for fingerprinting. They know all the angles. I say we bag it for tonight."

"That's got my vote," Alex said, "because the only thing we've come up with is that the son *might* want the land, for reasons we don't have a clue about. Maybe he wants to sell it and pick up some bucks. We couldn't prove it anyway. And who would give that kind of information to us kids?" He walked to the videocassette cabinet. "Let's watch *Indiana Jones*."

Robin was dumbfounded. She sat hugging her knees while they searched for the video. After all her work, all they could think about was a movie. She patted Rags' head, then began stuffing the papers back into the bags.

Alex heard the papers shuffling, looked over his shoulder and saw her face and shoulders sag. He looked at the piles of paper and thought of all the work she'd done. "You must have spent hours on that."

Robin nodded while stuffing the maps into the backpack, but didn't say a word.

"How about *Dr. Evil?*" he asked, holding his little finger to his lips to imitate Austin Powers.

"It's on Channel 3." Alex glanced at his watch. "There's still an hour left." He pushed the button on the remote and the screen lit up.

Robin fastened the buckle and dropped the bags onto the floor. She settled into the easy chair with Rags resting his head on her knee. Alex flipped through the channels. She stared at the screen. Marc and Alex laughed and mimicked Dr. Evil. It was stupid. Juvenile. She couldn't take anymore.

"Guys," she said, standing up, "I'm going to ride back to my house and get the computer games."

With a mouthful of popcorn Alex said, "You don't want to watch Austin?"

"Nah. I can't get into Austin now. I'll just ride to my house real quick and be back before the movie's over."

"You don't want us to go with you?" Marc asked above the noise of the movie.

"Nah. I need to think. Being by myself helps. I won't be long." She started to take the satchels but decided she could make the trip faster and easier without them, so she left them by the door.

Rags tried to follow her, but she pushed him back inside. "You have to stay, boy. I don't want you to get lost."

She paused at the door to wave at her friends, but they

were already absorbed in the movie. From the doorway she could hear Alex and Marc laughing. This hadn't been the big evening she thought it would be. In fact, it was a bust.

She closed the door, retrieved her bike, and rolled it down the drive. When she reached the street, everything seemed darker. She looked back at the house. Rags was standing at the window the way he was the day she found Seth missing. She had the urge to take him with her, but he might chase a cat or a coon and get lost in the fields and she would never forgive herself.

It seemed as if everything had gone wrong. Seth had been killed, Rags had lost his home and master. And her friends, well, they added up to a big zero right now.

She jumped onto her bike and pedaled to the corner. The fresh air felt good and she wasn't around her disappointing friends or stepfather. She was somewhere in-between and on her own. It felt good—till she turned onto Pike Road and saw the dark, lonely stretch of road between the cornfields.

Moonlight Chase

✳ ✳ ✳ ✳ ✳ ✳

Robin pedaled "Ol' Bob" in the dark. The boy's bike was named for her favorite uncle who had given it to her. The tires were worn, but it still rolled. She pedaled awhile, let the bike glide with its own momentum, then pedaled again. No reason to hurry. The guys would be watching the movie for at least an hour. Besides, she needed time to think. Think about the case, her friends, and her family.

The upside-down crescent moon that had caused so much trouble at her house was now a half-moon that ducked in and out of the clouds—like it was following her. The light shone through gaps in the clouds and fell heavy on her shoulders and back like a cold blanket. The effect was more like a set of headlights constantly behind her.

She thought of Marc and Alex and how they were always there when she needed them. That fact made their easy abandonment in the search for Seth's killer harder to take. After all, they owed it to Seth for all the wonderful things he'd done for them. The more she thought, the clearer it became. She really wasn't outgrowing her friends. She was just forgetting one basic fact—they were guys. They thought differently, and their heads sure were in a different place right now—on videos. Her head was on solving the murder, which she knew she could do if she could just nail down the motive.

As she felt the breeze on her face, she realized what really bothered her was not just their bailing out, but her feeling of failure. When it came to information, she had learned long ago that she could solve anything, even this case, with hard work. That's the way it was in school. Together they should have been able to figure out something, but Marc and Alex did nothing but throw in the towel at the first snag. It was just like their math class and everything else—they were expecting her to do all the work *and* provide the answers.

The more she thought about the amount of work she put into it and how little they did, the angrier she became. Soon she was standing on the pedals and pumping furiously. Sweat trickled down her forehead and onto her nose, causing her glasses to nearly slide off. She took a hand off the handlebar to push them back in place. The bike swerved hard to the right, sliding off the edge of the road. Air swooshed and within in seconds the rubber flapped along as the rim bounced over the gravel shoulder. She struggled to stop the bike and keep from crashing to the ground.

"What next?" she muttered as the bike finally stopped. The only thing she could do now was get off and start pushing it towards home.

She guided the bike down the road in the dim moonlight. An owl hooted soft and low. Three times? Or did the sound reverberate in the darkness? The air was different—still—now that she wasn't riding the bike. She stopped pushing and looked around. The stalks along the edge of the field were the only things she could make out. Beyond that, everything was a darkened blur. It was just her, the lonely road, whatever was beyond that first row of cornstalks, and that strange moon.

The rotten smell she had encountered before wafted on a light breeze. Great, she thought. That's all I need.

Pushing Ol' Bob with its lame tire became more of a chore than she thought. The flattened tire wobbled, hugging the road. At this rate, it would take all night to roll the two miles to her house. She looked for a place she could find again and saw an old bent fence post at the end of one corn row. She rolled the bike there, then into the field where it couldn't be seen from the road. Tomorrow, she'd have her mother drive back to get it.

As she laid the bike flat on the ground between two tall corn rows, she heard something shuffle. Her heart drummed in her chest. She was not alone. She squatted to listen.

Crickets chirped. A frog croaked. Something pressed through a row of stalks, rustling the dry husks. Then it rustled through another row. And another. Her skin felt as though ants were crawling on it. She wished she hadn't been so quick to leave Alex's house. It was a stupid, stupid thing to do.

After a long silence, she decided it had been a deer foraging for food. The area was loaded with them. Feeling calmer, she stood. The back of her neck prickled. That feeling again—that she wasn't alone. She bolted for the road, but caught her foot on something, and fell to the ground. Her glasses jettisoned into the darkness. She crawled around, feeling the dirt, straw, occasional stones, and God knows what else, trying to find them. Her hands felt coated in dirt. Then she noticed the chemical smell again, only stronger, causing her face to pucker and her eyes to burn. And a sound—a pulsing or pumping—like a mechanical heart. She stiffened. Glasses or no glasses, she was getting out of there. She jumped to her feet, bolted out of the cornfield, and hit the road at full speed. Fifty feet down the road she looked back and saw nothing following her. She had gotten away from the sound. Breathing hard, she slowed to a fast walk.

The road grew longer in the dark. If she ever got home, she'd never do something this stupid again. A cluster of hedge apple trees stood at the corner, blocking her view of the intersecting road. She passed the trees and turned the corner. Ahead, she saw two vehicles parked alongside the cornfield. One was a dark sedan, the other a tanker truck, and they were between her and home.

She mustered her courage and continued to walk toward the vehicles until she noticed something shiny snaking along the ground. She slowed for a better look and saw a thick metallic hose running from the truck into the field. *Why would a tanker truck be parked next to Seth's field in the middle of the night?* She stopped beside the car to check it out. It was empty, but the engine was idling. Suddenly, that foul odor hit her stronger than ever. It was definitely a chemical smell alright.

Cornstalks rustled. Footsteps! Two men were coming out of the cornfield, heading straight for the car. She ducked, but started breathing so hard she thought she would hyperventilate. Her bad luck was getting worse.

One of them said, "I'm leaving."

She hunched farther down and scooted to the back of the car where she crouched, gripping the cold, dusty bumper. Both men stopped.

"I'm not making any more trips." It was a southern drawl, like her Aunt May's in Kentucky.

"What do ya mean?" This voice was deep and coarse.

"Too risky. I'm out!"

"You're not gettin' out of anything!" The mean one shouted. He bumped the other guy against the car.

She felt the impact through her fingers on the bumper.

"You can't just walk out on me like that. Not now. We're partners, remember? Fifty-fifty. Money and work."

"Keep the money. I'm hittin' the road before things get any hotter."

"You're not going anywhere until the other loads are dumped!"

"Are you crazy? I didn't sign on for murder. They found the body! There could be someone snooping around here right now, for all we know."

Robin crouched lower to make herself smaller.

"Not at night, you fool. Not out here in the middle of nowhere." He was getting madder by the second. "I can't believe a kid found the body—and in hundreds of acres. I'd sure like to get my hands on him."

She nearly choked and pressed her hand over her mouth to muffle any sound. They were talking about Alex! And they *could* find him! His name was in all the newspapers. The more the mean guy talked, the madder he sounded. She gripped the bumper with both hands.

"You idiot. You buried him so a thirteen-year-old could find him! What'd you do, put a neon sign over the spot?"

"At least I wasn't stupid enough to kill him in the first place!"

She heard one man punch the other. Then they were grunting and scuffling against the car—getting closer.

She was trying to hide under the rear bumper when she touched the hot exhaust pipe. "Ahhh!" spilled from her mouth before she knew it.

The men stopped fighting.

"What was that?"

"Sounded like it came from the back of the car."

She jumped up and started running back down the road as fast as she could, glancing over her shoulder. She saw the men running, one behind the other—closing in. It wouldn't be long before they caught her. They were right on her heels by the time she saw the crooked fence post and made the quick turn into the cornfield. She hurdled the bike and raced down the row. She heard the men hit the bike in the dark, tumbling and thumping onto the ground.

Her feet pounded the earth. She was running on adrenaline and fear. She cut right, then left to get to the next row. She heard the men yell and threaten till their voices faded away. She ran faster than she ever had to the end of the field, and when she cleared it, she headed straight for Alex's house.

By the time she reached his porch steps, her legs felt like a weird combination of rubber and lead, and she could barely put one foot in front of the other. She grabbed the doorknob, turned it, and pressed her one-hundred-five pounds against it.

When Rags barked, Alex and Marc looked up to see

Robin stagger into the hallway. Her face was scarlet and her cheeks puffed in and out. She leaned against the wall, slid to the floor, and sat there in a heap.

"What happened, and where are your glasses?" Marc asked.

"Your face! It's—it's the color of your hair. And you're covered in dirt. Did you see a ghost or something? Talk to us!" Alex demanded, shaking her by the shoulders.

She trembled and tried to swallow, but couldn't. She licked dirt from her lips.

"Get her something to drink," Marc shouted. "She seems to be in shock or something." He patted her cheeks, but she shoved his hand away.

"Okay," Alex said, "but don't talk till I get back. I want to hear the whole story." He sprinted to the kitchen, jerked the refrigerator door open, and grabbed a can of Pepsi. He slammed the door with his hip and dashed back to the living room, popping the tab as he slid across the floor in his socks. Pepsi fizzed down the back of his hand.

"Now take a drink and talk!" Alex wiped his hand on his jersey.

"I know who killed Seth Dyer—and I know why!" she gasped.

Their eyes grew large and round. *She must have seen a ghost! Seth's?*

Alex looked toward the window, wondering what

answers she could have gotten out there in the dark. "How? I mean who?"

"Who?" she squeaked.

"Yes, who?" Alex and Marc said at the same time.

Her lips opened, then pursed. "I don't know."

Marc hung his thumbs in his pockets. "But you just said you did."

She shook her head. "Let me start at the beginning or you'll never understand." She swigged the Pepsi, wiping her mouth with the back of her hand.

Her words came in a rush. "When I left here, I took my bike, but when I got halfway down Port Road I had a flat." She pointed a finger at them. "This was all your fault, by the way."

Through clenched teeth Alex yelled, "Go on before I choke it out of you."

"You won't have to—the two men chasing me will do that."

Alex's jaw dropped.

Marc pulled back the curtain.

Robin grabbed his arm. "They'll see you. Get down!"

Marc dropped to the floor.

Robin reached up and locked the door.

"Who's chasing you?" Alex asked.

"Let me finish," Robin said. She told the rest of the story up to the point where she came into the house.

Alex gasped. "This gets better and better!"

"Better?" Marc said. "Are you crazy? They're out there somewhere riding around looking for Robin."

"Not just me. The real mean guy, the one who killed Seth, said he'd like to get his hands on the kid that found the body." She jabbed Alex's chest. "That's you! And your name was in *The Evening News*!"

Color drained from Alex's face.

Rags looked from one stunned face to the other and whined. Robin patted him.

"The way I see it," she said, "we've got to lay low for a while."

"Lay low my butt!" Alex said. "We've got to call the cops. They'll protect us. They'll put us in a witness protection program."

Marc slapped his forehead. "Witness protection program? *In Bridgeport?* Get real."

"He's right, Alex. If those guys want to get us, they will. There'll be no stopping them."

The room got real quiet.

Then Alex said, "I'm waking up Grandpa."

Only a Fool is Fearless
❉ ❉ ❉ ❉ ❉ ❉

Kota sat up on the edge of his bed listening to Marc, Alex, and Robin talk all at once. He glanced at the clock. It was nearly midnight. He raised his hand.

"*Ahpe*—wait! Please. I haven't caught a thing you've said except Robin's bicycle was killed and her glasses were kidnapped."

Robin looked at Marc and Alex. "He's close, really," she said.

Kota gave her a sideways glance while easing his feet into his bedroom moccasins. "Now, one at a time. Who's going first?"

Alex jumped in, "Robin left on her bike to get her Nintendo cartridges."

"At night? She didn't go by herself?"

Alex looked away as Marc looked down.

"Are you kids crazy?"

Kota always seemed bigger when he was angry. Alex

elbowed Robin. "Why don't you tell him the rest?"

Robin drew in a breath and repeated the story.

Kota listened patiently as he led them to the kitchen to make hot chocolate. When she got to the part about the men, Kota turned from the stove. "Why didn't you tell me that sooner?"

Robin became mute and stared. Then she found her tongue, "I, uh, tried."

"Make sure the doors are locked, boys. And the windows. Draw the curtains. Then come right back to the kitchen. Kota grabbed the wall phone and called the sheriff's home number. A sleepy Roy Newby answered.

"Roy, this is Kota. Yes, Bear Sanders. I'm sorry to wake you, but you need to get an officer out to Port Road right away and another one here to Karen's." He filled him in as the kids listened to his side of the conversation. "Yes. When they realized Robin heard them. Correct. They chased her. Could be outside now."

Kota hung up and patted Robin's shoulder. "The sheriff's on his way."

Kota went to the den and unlocked the gun cabinet.

"You're getting Dad's gun?" Alex asked.

"I'm just making sure they're not loaded."

He strapped on his twelve-inch knife in its leather sheath.

Marc and Robin exchanged looks.

"We're safe here with Grandpa. He's fearless," Alex

whispered to them, "That's another reason ol' Sheriff Woodward got Grandpa to help track people."

"I told you, *Mitakoja*, only a fool is fearless."

Kota hustled back to the kitchen with Rags and them following closely like ducklings in a row.

"Now listen carefully," Kota said, peering around the kitchen curtain. "I want you three to go back into the den, turn off all the lights, and turn up the volume on the TV. Then go to the bathroom, lock the door, and sit on the floor. Do not turn on the light. There's a flashlight under the sink if you need it. You can leave on the hall light if you want. I'm going outside."

"Outside?" Robin grabbed his shirt with both hands. "Are you crazy? They're out there. Stay in here with us behind locked doors."

"I will watch the house from up in the white oak. From there I will have hawk's eyes. No one will see me, but I will see anything that comes near the house and yard."

"But Grandpa, there are two of them."

"I can handle it. Now do as I say and don't leave the bathroom for any reason. Understand?" He waited for each to nod.

When they were safely in the bathroom, Kota slipped out of Alex's bedroom window, crouched low in the shrubs, and seeing no one, hurried to the tree and climbed up. From that vantage point in the branches, he watched the road, most of the yard, and the glass doors to the den where the TV cast a faint, flickering light through the curtains.

Ten long minutes later, two Bridgeport police cars screeched to a halt in front of the house and shone spotlights over the yard. The sheriff and two deputies got out of the cars with guns drawn and started across the grass.

Kota cautiously watched them begin to search. They walked below him, split up, and searched the back yard. Never once did they look up into the tree. If he had been an enemy or a four-legged hunting for food, they would be dead. The three men holstered their guns and walked to the front where they rang the doorbell.

Knowing the kids were locked in the bathroom, Kota slid down the tree and called out, "Don't shoot, it's me, Kota. I'm coming around the house to let you in."

When Kota stepped into the light, the sheriff said, "Good thing ya warned us. Rusty here's so jumpy he'd have made Swiss cheese of you."

"What did you find on Port Road?" Kota said as he unlocked the door.

"Nothing. Guess they took off. We'll check for tire prints tomorrow in the daylight." He turned to the deputy. "Rusty, you stay outside to keep an eye out. Jake, you come in with me."

Rusty nodded as they went inside.

"Where are the kids?" the sheriff asked.

Kota got the kids and Rags from their hiding place.

Robin told the story again for the sheriff and his deputy.

"Big dark car," the sheriff repeated. "That describes half the cars in the county. Any idea what make or model?"

Robin shook her head. "No. It was just dark. Black or maybe dark blue. Anything really. Couldn't tell in the dark."

The sheriff tapped his hat against his leg. "Okay. If I understand this correctly, you were crouched down behind the car, right? You must have been eyeball to eyeball with the license plate. Do you remember the number?"

Ten eyes stared at Robin, twelve counting Rags', making it hard for her to think.

'The Brain' would know, Alex thought. He'd bet his allowance on the number spilling from her lips in 2.5 seconds.

"I told you I lost my glasses, and it was dark. I couldn't see much of anything."

Alex's head shook. The one time 'Ms. Know It All' really needed to, she didn't.

"But it was an Indiana tag," she said suddenly, "and not from Kirk County."

"Why do you say that?" the sheriff asked.

"Well, I noticed the county name looked different. It didn't say 'Kirk.' It was a longer name and I strained to see it. Ooh—what was it?" She hit her fist on the arm of the chair.

"Jefferson! That's it. Jefferson County."

"That's up around Madison," the deputy said.

"That's where Seth's son lives," Marc said. "What was his name?"

"Sonny," Alex said.

"That cinches it," Robin said. "He's the killer. He had motive and now his car has been placed at the scene. I even heard the confession!"

"Now kids," the sheriff said, "don't be jumping to conclusions. Living in a city's not a crime. Never has been. And that's all we've got because thousands of people own big, dark cars and live in Madison."

He stood. "May be a coincidence, but certainly one worth looking into. We'll pay Sonny Dyer a little visit." He turned for the door. "I'll also check with the D.M.V. tomorrow—see what kind of car he drives."

Robin whispered to Marc and Alex. "That's the Division of Motor Vehicles."

"We know," Marc huffed.

Kota stopped the sheriff at the door. "These men may already know where my grandson lives. And as Robin said, they want to get their hands on the boy who found the body. We can't take any chances."

The sheriff looked at the kids. "I guess I don't have to tell you three to be real careful till we find these guys. My call is, they'd be more interested in the one who overheard them confessing to the murder."

Robin's shoulders sagged. *Oh! That made her feel better.*

"What will you do to protect them?" Kota said.

"I'll have someone watch the house as much as I can," he said. "Problem is, I only have three deputies and there are three kids to watch, along with the rest of Bridgeport and everything that goes on every day. So about all I can do is rotate one officer between the houses."

"They'll be at school most of the day," Kota offered. "So just cover the time after they get home till they leave the next morning. They catch the bus between 7:55 and 8:05 in the mornings and return around 3:45. I can pick up each one in the morning for school, but I can't pick them up in the afternoons."

"That'll help, Kota," the sheriff said. He looked at Marc. "You're Corby's son, aren't you?"

"Yes sir." It wasn't a hard guess since his was the only African-American family in the small town of Bridgeport.

"You live right across the street, right?"

Marc nodded.

Sheriff Newby turned to Jake. "Since he lives across the street, we're really just talking two locations, here and Maple, where the girl lives. I want you and Rusty to rotate afternoons. Got it?" Jake nodded. "Hopefully, having the squad cars drive by everyday will deter them. If not, then there's not much more I can do."

Telling the Truth
✳ ✳ ✳ ✳ ✳ ✳

At lunch on Saturday Kota, Marc, Alex, and Robin were eating corn dogs and chips when the sheriff called. He said his deputies had scoured the cornfield, but found no evidence anyone had been there, not even Robin. No sign of a bicycle or glasses—not even a footprint.

Robin's eyes were wide with astonishment.

"Perhaps you checked the wrong spot," Kota said. "I'll bring Robin right over to show you where it was." He hung up the phone. "Finish your dogs and get your shoes on, kids. The sheriff needs your help."

Minutes later, Kota eased his black '74 pick-up to the side of the road behind the sheriff's car. The sheriff and his deputies got out to meet them. Kota spoke to the sheriff while Robin looked along the road for the crooked fence post.

"There it is," she said, pointing to the post. "That's the row. I left my bike there because the post would make it easy to find."

She hurried into the cornfield, but stopped when she didn't see her bike. Her eyes scanned the ground while she turned in all directions. She looked back to the post. It was the same row. It didn't make any sense. She shook her head and knelt down to hunt for the glasses. She looked under leaves and cornhusks and searched adjacent rows, both east and west. To her dismay, there was nothing but dirt, debris, and cornstalks.

"I left them right here," she said, pointing to the ground. "I know it was here because of the fence post. And when I ran back here in the dark, I jumped over the bike and they tripped on it. That's how I got away." She pressed her temples with her fingers.

The sheriff spat a brown stream near her foot.

"They've got to be here somewhere," she insisted. "You have to believe me."

"We believe you," Marc said. He and Alex started searching the stalks, hoping the glasses might have hung in one. They searched the area for fifteen minutes before finally giving up.

"Since Robin can't see as well without her glasses," Kota said, "I want you and Marc to search again and see what you can find." Kota walked into the field, too.

"This *is* the right row!" Robin insisted to the sheriff. "They—they must have taken them. That's the only explanation. They took the bicycle *and* the glasses."

"They found the glasses in the dark?" the sheriff asked.

Robin stared at him. It was a good question. "They must have had a flashlight with them."

"Honey," the sheriff said while hitching his gun belt, "the ground is clean. My yard's not this clean. And there's no footprints, no tire tracks, and no glasses. This is all a big mistake, unless your bicycle and glasses sprouted wings and flew out of the cornfield."

What could she say? She stared at the cornstalks.

The sheriff stepped closer. "Now, understand this is serious business. Police officers don't have the time to be running around playing peek-a-boo games in a cornfield."

"I'm not playing games, Sheriff Newby." She crossed her arms. "And I'm not making this up. I was nearly kidnapped and could have been killed out here last night! Oooh." She stamped her foot. "This is so frustrating. The bike and glasses were here. I was here. That's all I know."

"Young lady, let me give you the actual facts. You said there was a tanker truck and a car out here last night, but we can't find any tracks to substantiate that. We have a car that routinely rides by here during the night. That officer said he never saw nothing."

"Well, I didn't see any police car, either. Wish I had. Then you'd believe me—I think."

"Also," the sheriff said, ignoring her, "something the size of a tanker truck should have left some kind of imprint—tire tracks or something. But there's nothing. We combed every inch of where you said the truck and car were supposed to be and the only thing we found was a rotten smell. And if you ask me, this whole thing smells rotten. There's no bicycle with a flat tire, no glasses that are red or green or any other color of the rainbow." He was almost yelling in her face now and his breath was like a tobacco sewer.

She backed away.

When she didn't say anything, he said, "So what do you think? Could this be the wrong *cornfield*? The wrong planet? Or do ya think maybe—just maybe, you dreamed the whole thing up?"

Robin's face flushed and she ran to Kota's truck.

Marc was livid. "Robin doesn't lie, Sheriff, and this was no dream. You didn't see her when she first got back last night. She was terrified. If she said something happened out here last night, then you can—"

"Or maybe your friend just felt left out of the party and wanted some attention. She did leave the house all alone, right? Maybe she got spooked out here all by herself and made up the story about being chased so you wouldn't think she was afraid of the dark. She had to come up with something when she didn't come back with the games."

Kota returned as Alex and Marc stormed off to join Robin now sitting on the front bumper of his truck.

"It's okay, Robin," Alex said. "We know you're telling

the truth. He's just a jerk. He wouldn't know a clue or an eyewitness if one bit him in the butt."

She stared down at her shoes without saying a word.

The sheriff told his deputies to load up, but Kota stopped him in his path.

Marc saw him and elbowed his friends.

"She's telling the truth, Roy," Kota said, looking down at the sheriff with narrowed eyes.

The kids slipped into the field a few rows over to listen.

"Sometimes you have to follow your gut," Kota said.

The kids squatted down.

"And my instinct tells me she's not lying. She was in real trouble out here last night and we're very lucky nothing happened to her."

"Oh, really?" the sheriff twisted his lips to the side and glanced at Rusty. "Then tell me this. Just how am I going to write *that* on my report? Should I say, 'There's absolutely no evidence to prove anything ever happened out there, *but* in my heart,' he held his hand over his heart, 'I believe this kid is telling the truth.'"

Rusty snickered.

The sheriff started around Kota, but he grabbed the man's elbow. "Just a minute, Roy. You said you couldn't find anything, right?"

"Yeah. What of it?"

"If you examined the area, then you should have noticed

it's a little too smooth, brushed in fact, while ten feet in any direction the ground is covered with deer and rodent tracks."

The sheriff opened his mouth to talk, but Kota cut him off. "And what about the chemical smell? It's never been here before. Doesn't it seem odd that a chemical odor lingers in the exact spot where Robin said a tanker truck had its hose stretched into the field?"

Marc whispered, "Gotcha!"

"And if I were the sheriff," Kota said, "I'd sure hate to get a call from the county health officials, possibly the Mayor, asking why I failed to get a soil sample when I knew full well the ground might be contaminated with toxic waste. That'd be real hard to explain, now wouldn't it, Roy?"

Newby's face grew red. The last thing he needed was for the Mayor to accuse him of sloppy police work, or for Dr. McCracken to say he ignored public health threats. He spat.

"How about it, Sheriff? Is the possibility of soil contamination something you could and should write down in your report?"

"Now look, Kota, you know how it is. Kids are making prank calls all the time. And I don't know that kid." He shook his head. "She could be okay or she could be trouble. I've got a police department to run and I can't be jumping up every time a kid claims to see a ghost or something."

"She's a citizen of this town, like everybody else," Kota reminded him.

The sheriff shot Rusty an irritated look. "Give the area another once-over and report back to me. And I want a soil sample taken over to McCracken A.S.A.P."

The sheriff returned to his car, stomped his shoes on the blacktop, got in, and sped away.

From two rows over, the kids quietly high-fived. Without looking behind him, Kota said, "Load up you three. We're heading home."

Marc asked, "How did he know—?"

"Load up—we have to get away from these chemicals."

Robin took his hand. "Thanks for standing up for me."

"Don't worry, Robin. You have a good heart. Everything will work out."

"I can't get Seth off my mind," she said. "I hope the sheriff can find the killers."

"I do, too," Alex said as they walked past the deputy.

As Rusty knelt down to fill some plastic bags with soil, he watched Kota and the kids load into the truck and drive away. His eyes narrowed. He wasn't about to let some darn Injun and a bunch of bratty kids run the show. After they drove off, he dumped the soil from the bags, stuffed them in his pockets, and headed back to his car. Another half-mile down the road he stopped and filled the bags with different soil. He returned to the police station and stuffed the bag in the bottom drawer of his desk.

Witness Tattooed on His Forehead
✳ ✳ ✳ ✳ ✳ ✳

Kota drove Marc and Robin home, then returned to Alex's house where he spent the rest of the day at the window watching the road between the intersection and the dead end.

"You've been awfully quiet in here," Karen said, joining him. "You're looking for those men, aren't you?" He nodded. "But why are you watching the dead end? They'd have to drive in from the other direction."

"If they come by car."

Karen stiffened. The area behind the house and the dead end was continuous woods. Beyond that was the forty-acre field that ran beside the Corby's house. She felt for a chair and sat down.

"The police are riding by, right?"

"Yes."

"But you think the men might come through the woods or through Corby's field?"

"It's possible." He rubbed his hands down his face. "I don't want to frighten you Karen, but I don't think we should count on the sheriff and his deputies."

She tensed and began rubbing her arms.

"What I mean is, they're busy and understaffed. If they get an emergency call when they're supposed to be here, they'll have to respond."

"But these are killers, Dad. I'd consider that an emergency. Especially since they might come after Alex."

"They won't harm him," Kota said. "I'll make sure of that."

"But you can't be with him twenty-four hours a day, every day."

"No. But there's safety in numbers and those kids stick together. I don't think those guys'll try anything with the three of them. They'd be too much to handle."

"Look! There's a squad car now," Karen said, walking to the window. The car cruised slowly by, turned around at the cul-de-sac and headed out. Kota decided not to tell her it was the first he'd seen of them.

That night, outside Madison, Indiana, Frank Cooper walked into Dixie's Tavern. He took the back booth and ordered a beer. A country singer whined from the jukebox that somebody done her wrong, but he wasn't listening. He tilted the frosty mug and let the brew pool in his mouth before sliding down his throat. As he lowered his mug onto the table, he saw Buster McClain wander into the restaurant, wearing the same coveralls and green flannel shirt he had worn the day before. He was a slender five-feet-ten-inches tall, and his mousy brown hair looked wind blown. Being a snappy dresser himself, keeping the company of the country-bumpkin grated on his nerves.

Cooper raised his hand to let Buster know where he was and grabbed a fistful of peanuts from the basket, cracked some, and tossed them into his mouth. His temple throbbed as he watched Buster take his time getting to the booth. Every time the jerk stopped to talk to someone, Cooper cracked the nuts a little harder. Before long he was just cracking out of frustration—without eating.

He hadn't known Buster long, but prided himself on knowing an opportunity when he saw one. When he over-heard the doofus talking about how much money could be made disposing of toxic wastes, Cooper had known he had to strike a deal with this creep.

He recalled how easy it had been to get Buster to talk. After just a few minutes, he knew the guy was simple-mind-ed. He'd heard him talking with Stanley Edwards about the factory having trouble with environmental geeks. The geeks were questioning the way the automotive parts factory dis-posed of PERC. PERC, he learned, after he bought Buster a few drinks, was a toxic liquid the company used in manufacturing rubber tires.

The way he figured it, the factory wouldn't mind paying someone to get rid of that messy problem. He just needed to work out the details and make the right contacts. After all, he wasn't going to soil *his* hands. He needed a driver. And Buster had a septic tank pumper he called "The Honey Dipper." He also had access to trucks at the plant since he worked there. And the biggest bonus of all, he already knew how to falsify environmental disposal records. Buster, Cooper decided, was his man.

Buster had gotten too drunk to drive that night, so he drove the jabber-mouth to the trailer. It was on that drive that he formulated the plan in his mind. By the time he left Buster's place, they had set up a meeting for the next day so they could discuss the "sober" details.

By the end of the next evening, he had talked Buster into a partnership. He would be the brain of the operation and would create a plan and collect the money. Buster would do the labor and use his tanker to dispose of the toxic waste. They would split it fifty-fifty. Roughly $200,000. That made a cool $100,000 each. That was the plan, for now anyway.

Cooper rubbed his whitened knuckles. He reminded himself of what he had riding on the deal if he could just be patient. He traced the pink scar on the side of his face with his finger and waited.

At the table, Buster removed his faded army jacket and hooked it on the peg by the booth. He hadn't changed from his work clothes and his hands were covered in grime. Cooper wanted to puke. Cleanliness was important to him, had been since he was a child. He had to have clean clothes, a clean car, a clean house, and clean hands—especially clean hands. Buster's fingernails looked like he'd been digging potatoes with them. No telling what kind of bacteria was growing under them. But he could tolerate him till the project was finished, which wouldn't be long.

Buster flashed a toothy grin as the jukebox switched CD's and Willie Nelson started crooning. "How ya doin', partner?" he said, swinging his hips to the beat. "Don't ya just love that Willie Nelson?"

Cooper's mouth remained set.

Buster's smile faded as he looked into Cooper's very dark eyes. Shark eyes, cold, and predatory. The pink scar etched from his left ear down through his beard was obviously a signature of a darker past. Buster knew little about him, but the look on his face said it wasn't the time to chat about the guy's family history.

With the exception of the scar, Cooper was a good-looking man who could charm a "yes" out of anyone, especially the ladies. Buster had seen him do that on several occasions.

He was also fussy about his clothes, which according to him, were tailor-made. He was a dandy all right, especially with that huge diamond earring in his left ear. That was the extent of what Buster knew about Frank Cooper—he was demanding, too perfect, and too particular. It was irritating to a laid-back person like him.

Cooper finished lining up his silverware and answered Buster's question. "I'll tell you how it's going, partner." His voice was sharp. "It's actually going pretty bad. We still have two loads to dump and our dump site is now crawling with the cops. And to make matters worse, we have a pint-sized witness running around. One who can identify us as—" He looked over his shoulder, "murderers."

"I didn't murder nobody. You—"

"Keep your voice down, you fool!" Cooper snapped, looking around. "Use your head. I keep telling you that. When are you going to learn?"

"Well, if I'm supposed to be using my head, why did *you* tell me to meet ya at a truck stop? Especially if you're so worried about somebody hearing us. We could have met at my place or yours."

"I wouldn't go to that pigsty trailer of yours again," Cooper said, wetting his napkin in the glass of water and wiping a spot on the table.

"It was sure good enough for you when you were trying to talk me into this little deal. And, I repeat—" he leaned closer across the table and looked into his eyes. "I didn't murder nobody. *You* did the murdering."

To Cooper, Buster suddenly had the word *witness* tattooed across his forehead. Maybe he would have to eliminate him, too. But he'd wait until after the last tanker was dumped and the money was collected from the factory. A $200,000 payoff was twice as good as what he'd get if Buster was still walking around. For now he'd keep the idiot happy, so he wouldn't walk.

"Maybe that's true, but just remember, you *are* an accessory—and that spells jail time. So let's follow the plan and not make any mistakes. I'll tell you what," Cooper said, forcing a smile, "let's order a big, juicy prime rib. In fact, order the eighteen-ouncer with the works—I'll even pay for it. Order some grog to wash it down. While we eat, we'll figure out what to do about the kid."

Buster was uneasy. Frank's eyes were so dark he couldn't tell where the pupils ended. But the idea of the eighteen-ouncer sure sounded good—especially if Cooper was paying for it. "Grog too, you say?"

Cooper smiled and signaled the waitress.

"What'll you have?" Her blonde pony tail bounced.

He read the white plastic name badge. "Julie."

"That's my name." She tapped her name badge with the eraser of her pencil while waiting for the order. He was a study in black. Black hair, black beard, black eyes. As an art student, she had the urge to draw him. Especially with that long curved scar trailing into his closely-cut, neat beard. Different clothes and he'd look like a pirate. She noticed the earring.

"Whoa! That's some rock you're wearing," Julie said, admiring it. "What's that—two, maybe three karats?"

Cooper grinned. "Three point one-two, to be exact."

"It's a beauty." She flipped a page on her tablet, standing with her pencil poised above it. "What can I get you?"

Frank studied her. She was a perky little thing, with blonde hair, blue eyes and a small mouth. "I haven't seen you in here before. I'd remember a face like yours, Goldilocks. You new?"

"No, but you must be. I've been waiting these tables here for six years. You must have been here when I was on vacation last week." She cocked her head to the side. "And what brings a smooth-talking guy like you to a honky-tonk place like this?" She learned long ago to make the customers feel good. It yielded better tips.

Cooper winked. "You."

He ordered big steaks for both of them, then folded his arms and said, "So tell me, Miss Julie, how late do you work tonight?"

She slid her pencil into her hair over her ear. "It's *Mrs.* Julie, and I work until my husband picks me up."

She turned on her heel and headed for the kitchen. She

had to put up with a lot at Dixie's, but she would be graduating from college soon and all of this would be behind her.

When Julie brought more drinks, Cooper said, "Your husband works a night shift?"

"Yeah."

He shot a glance at Buster. "Does he work at the tire factory?"

"Nope," she said, scooping peanut shells from the table.

"Then he's a fireman or a cop," he said, trying to keep the conversation going so he could learn more about her.

"Nope. If you must know, he's a conservation officer. Actually, he can arrest a cop if it came down to it—or even a customer for that matter," she said, smiling smugly. Another customer signaled her and she walked away.

"Guess you can't win 'em all, huh Frank?"

Cooper tapped the frosty mug and said nothing.

By the time they finished, Buster had not only eaten the entire steak dinner, fat and all, but had downed six beers and a big piece of apple pie, which he capped off with a last brew. He also made four trips to the restroom. By eleven o'clock, Cooper had convinced him to finish the remaining jobs.

"So what about the kid?" Buster asked.

"I haven't heard anything on the news, which is good. But we have to assume she told her parents. That means it's probably been reported. The bottom line is that we have to find her. At least we have the bike and, to our good fortune, it has an I.D. tag on it. I can get a girlfriend of mine who works down at the police department to look up the kid's name and address. I should have it first thing Monday morning. We'll go from there."

"It was a good thing the glasses were caught in the spokes or we might have missed 'em in the dark," Buster said, snagging a fistful of peanuts. "By the way, where's the bike now?"

Cooper looked him in the eyes. "If I told ya, I'd have to kill ya."

Buster stopped chewing and swallowed the mouthful of nuts.

Cooper laughed, stood, and slapped Buster on the shoulder. "Just kidding. Behind my garage. Looks pretty worn out, too. Losing it might be the best thing that ever happened to that kid."

Cooper pulled out a money clip of neatly folded bills and slipped out some twenties. He calculated the tip and threw in a few extra bucks so Julie would remember him. When she arrived to pick up the money, he motioned he didn't need change. She flashed a big smile and he watched her legs as she walked back to the register.

When she was out of sight, Cooper said, "What'd you do with the glasses?"

"They're in my tanker truck."

Cooper stared at him. "You're riding around with those

things? Buster, you have to get them out of your truck. We can't have somebody finding them. Hide them somewhere else! You understand?"

"Now who's gonna be looking through my truck?"

"Thanks to that pipsqueak, the cops probably know about it," Cooper said, trying to quell his anger.

"Oh, guess you're right," Buster said. He scratched his head. "At least I got the tractor back to the farmer's house."

"Good. It gives the police less to work with."

They headed for the door where they shook hands and said goodnight. Buster drove off, but Cooper slipped back into the restroom to wash his hands. He scrubbed them twice and pushed open the door with his elbow. He had to be careful about a lot of things, now—his dim-witted friend and the kid. Either one of them could land him in jail—a place he couldn't revisit. He could play Buster along—no problem. But the kid. He would have to take care of her himself.

Unfamiliar Territory

✳ ✳ ✳ ✳ ✳ ✳

First thing Monday morning, Kota picked up the kids and dropped them off at school as promised. Then he drove to the courthouse to see a friend who worked in the County Clerk's office. After visiting three city or county offices, Kota was convinced there was no plan to build on Seth's land. The kids would be disappointed.

Robin went through the lunch line before Marc and Alex and located a table with three empty seats. She set down her tray and placed books on each of the other seats to save them. Before sitting down she waved to Marc and Alex who were still in the line.

Marc had already spotted her tousled hair in the crowd. He nodded, so she sat down and started eating her pizza while it was still hot. Unfortunately, Marc was not the only one who noticed her.

Brad Skeemer and his friends, Doug and Charlie, were

ahead of Marc and Alex in line. Charlie tapped Brad on the shoulder and pointed to Robin.

"Look at that hair," Charlie said. "Looks like she stuck her finger in a light socket."

Doug quipped, "It just looks like a burning bush to me."

Brad lifted his bottle of lemonade. "I could put it out."

Brad and his friends made their way through the tables till they were ten feet from Robin. Brad handed his tray to Doug, took the thirty-two-ounce bottle of pink lemonade off the tray and removed the cap. He stepped directly behind Robin, who was eating and never saw him.

Marc looked in Robin's direction and saw Brad tilt the bottle over her head. But before he could yell, pink liquid cascaded off her head onto her face and clothes and swamped her tray.

Robin screamed and jumped straight up, knocking over her chair.

Brad jumped back, laughing so hard he could barely stand up.

"Just putting out that burning bush, girl." Brad said, as though he were doing her a favor.

Students all over the cafetorium broke into raucous laughter while Robin stood with soggy tendrils clinging to her face.

She parted the hair in her face with her fingers and glared at Brad, pink lemonade dripping from her nose and chin. Her *Save the Rain Forest* T-shirt was drenched. The hair on her arms stuck to her skin. Tidal waves of emotions crashed inside her while kids laughed and pointed. She could just die.

She looked down at her pizza floating in pink lemonade. Without thinking twice, she picked up the paper plate and slapped the soggy mess into Brad's face.

Brad stood as still as an anvil while the mushy pizza slid down his face and plopped onto the tile floor. Doug and Charlie laughed as hard as everyone else. Brad glared at them, grabbing napkins from his tray and wiping his reddening face. He lunged for Robin.

She backed against the table, but he grabbed her shoulder with one hand and drew back his fist. Marc dropped his tray and snatched Brad's hand in midair. He spun him around and punched him in the nose like a professional boxer. Brad sailed backwards into Charlie and Doug, causing the three of them to tumble down the stairs to the lower level. Trays of food clanged along after them.

Alex had Marc's back, standing with his fists up, prepared for opposition.

A deep voice bellowed above the commotion. "What's going on here?" It was Miss Pitts, the principal, standing with her hands propped on her hips. She eyeballed Marc's fists.

"Just because you look like Mohammed Ali," she said, wagging a warning finger in his face, "doesn't mean you have to act like him. That will get you nothing but trouble."

Amy Scholer quickly offered a hurried account.

"That creep Brad Skeemer dumped lemonade all over Robin and her food, so she shoved her pizza in his face. Then Brad was going to punch her! That's when Marc stopped him and punched him. Then those guys tumbled down the steps like the Three Stooges." She grinned, seemingly waiting for applause.

"Is that right?" Miss Pitts asked, looking at the others for confirmation. They nodded. Miss Pitts looked at Robin.

"Are you okay, honey?" she asked, bending down and looking sympathetically into Robin's eyes.

What could she say? My life is a toilet and you could do me a favor by flushing it! She couldn't say what she really felt—not with everybody watching. She just shrugged.

"Looks like you need some dry clothes, honey. Do you have another shirt in your locker?" The tall principal was bending over Robin, making her feel smaller.

The shirt in her locker wasn't what she'd classify as dry since she'd just had PE, but she nodded again. She just wanted to get out of there, away from all the staring eyes, and end this nightmare.

"Then go get changed and when you get back we'll see about getting you some more food."

The last thing in the world Robin wanted to do was come back to the lunchroom. "Thanks, Miss Pitts, but I'm not hungry now."

Miss Pitts turned to Brad and his friends. "And you boys," she said, pointing a long finger. "And *you*." To Robin's horror she pointed to Marc. "Come with me." She turned on her heel and stormed off with the four of them following.

As Marc passed, Robin touched his arm and whispered, "I'm so sorry." She watched him walk towards the principal's office with his head down. She felt as though she would lose her mind. Her life was bad enough, but now she was ruining her friend's life as well. She looked around. Everyone was still staring at her. She bolted for the gymnasium.

"Robin!" Alex called. When she didn't stop, he chased after her. He ran into the gymnasium, across the basketball court, and out the back door before catching up with her. He found her sitting on the sidewalk, her knees drawn up to her chest, her arms folded tightly around them, and her back rising and falling as she rocked.

He let the door go and as soon as it clanged shut, he realized they were locked out. That didn't matter. Sobbing Robin was what mattered. He'd never seen her like this. The Robin he knew was always in control. He leaned against the wall and slid down to sit beside her.

"That was a rotten thing Brad did."

She looked across the parking lot as she wiped her tears. Her face was double sticky with bitter salty tears and sugary-sweet lemonade.

"People hate me."

Alex couldn't believe what he heard. "No, they don't. And if by *people* you mean Brad Skeemer, well, he's not even human."

"Yes, they do hate me."

"That's not true." She was like a wounded bird and it broke his heart to see her like that. "Robin, don't you see?"

She looked at him with watery eyes.

"They just wish they could be like you. And since they can't, they try to tear you down. They want to make you— less you. Don't let them do it."

Robin wiped her nose with the back of her hand. Alex turned away. *This was why the guys in movies carried handkerchiefs.* When he looked back, she didn't seem any better.

"I wish I could be *half* of what you are, Robin. But I'm not and I never will be."

Robin looked at him. "You're so much more, Alex. You're popular, and athletic, and cute."

"Well, that's true," Alex joked.

Robin managed a weak grin.

"Which do you think will go farther in life, Robin? Your brains or my popularity?"

She shook her head. "Being like you goes a long way, Alex, and you know it."

"Robin, you're smart and you're liked a lot. You seem to forget that there's only one person who treats you badly.

One person, Robin!" He held one finger to her face. "Brad Skeemer. He's like a pirate—a pirate who likes to steal people's joy. And it doesn't matter what that slime ball thinks anyway, now does it?"

She didn't answer.

"No! It doesn't," he said. "You've got to get the right perspective on this. You're forgetting all the other people who think you're incredible."

Alex heard himself. *What was he saying?* He was stepping over a line between acting like a kid and acting like an adult. It was new territory, like wearing grown-up clothes that were way too big. It was time to cut it short.

"Robin, you can't let one person ruin your life. Especially a twit like Brat Skeemer."

Robin sniffed and wiped a last tear. She looked at Alex. She wanted to say something but didn't know what. He was the nicest person she had ever known. And the cutest. And, she really liked him, a lot, but wouldn't dare say it. She looked at her hands while rubbing the dried lemonade. Telling him how she felt could ruin everything. And their friendship was one of the most important things in her life. It was best left unsaid—at least for now.

She lightly punched his knee. "Thanks for being such a good friend. You have no idea how much it means."

A Killer Gets Close

✷ ✷ ✷ ✷ ✷ ✷

After the cafetorium incident, Mr. Michaels confirmed to Ms. Pitts that Marc was indeed protecting Robin. He also vouched for his character. As a result, the principal let him off the hook with just a lecture on the evils of fighting. Brad, on the other hand, received a week's detention, and his friends had to write essays about why they shouldn't make fun of others.

Life at Bridgeport School returned to normal by the next day. Robin's hair was tamed by a braid and she was her usual studious, compulsive, and upbeat self. Marc's heroic deed for Robin was the hot topic around school and everyone wanted to high-five him.

Alex's life was another story. It was a roller coaster flying off the tracks. Every time he saw Allie, Jed was with her and he hated that. He also hated feeling like the outsider and finally stopped talking when he ran into them.

During a class change, Allie said, "Hey Alex. Don't you speak anymore?"

Jed stopped babbling and acted surprised Alex was even on the planet.

"Oh, hi Allie. How's it going?"

She glanced at Jed, then back to Alex. "So so."

Alex looked from her to Jed. "Guess I better get to class. See ya." Then he headed down the hall.

"See ya," she said softly, watching Alex disappear into C-wing.

"Allie. Have you listened to anything I've said?" Jed demanded.

"Huh? Oh yeah. Your dad's taking you somewhere."

"Not just somewhere. To a U of L ball game. Duh. I swear, Allie, where's your head?"

She wanted to tell him. Instead, she held up her hand and said, "I have to go now. Catch ya later." She scurried through the crowd and ducked into the bathroom where she leaned against the wall, thankful to be rid of Jed and his ten-gallon ego. She wet a paper towel and held it to her face. A toilet flushed in one of the stalls and Monica walked out.

"What's wrong with you?" Monica asked.

Allie tossed the towel into the waste bin. "I'm so sick of that Jed I could barf."

"At least somebody's interested in you—and a quarterback no less."

"But he's so—uncool. I wish he were more like Alex. *He's* got it all. Only problem is, he doesn't give me the time of day."

"Alex?" Monica said as she washed her hands. "That's easy. Just get to know Robin. They're buds from way back and they're always together."

Allie remembered Robin mentioning the Math Club. "Really? That's not a bad idea. Thanks, Mon."

During the 5th period class change, Marc noticed Robin staring into her locker. He started to ask what she was doing when someone nearby yelled out. He turned and saw Brad Skeemer back away from a landslide of gerbil pellets streaming onto his feet. The mound of food made him look planted to the spot. Students laughed, crowding into the bay to get a better view.

Monica's shrill voice rose above the laughter. "B-r-r-rat's got r-r-rat food in his locker!"

Brad got in her face. "Shut up, you screechy—whatever!"

Robin closed her locker door without once looking towards the commotion. She leaned Marc's way and pressed a crumpled ten-dollar bill into his hand.

"Would you give this to Mr. Whiskers for me?" She winked and sashayed down the hall.

During math class, Allie asked when the first Math

Club meeting would be. Ms. Newton explained it would meet on the first and third Tuesdays after school, which meant it wouldn't start until the following week. She then asked if anyone needed tutoring before that time.

Robin looked at Alex. He was watching Allie. It was clear he wanted Allie's attention. He might even suffer through extra math problems to get it, but he was keeping his mouth shut and his hand down.

Finally, Robin said, "Alex raised his hand."

His arm slid off his desk as he glared at her.

Ms. Newton smiled and said, "Really, Alex?"

The cat was out of the bag. "Uh, yes ma'am. But I couldn't stay long."

Then Ms. Newton asked who would be willing to tutor him. He gripped the edge of his seat. No one spoke, so she asked Robin.

Robin couldn't believe her ears. She would do it in a heartbeat. But this wasn't for her. It was for Alex. Her mind raced. "Since I lost my glasses, I've been wearing my old ones. Things are blurry. I better pass."

Alex saw Monica look his way and her hand began rising into the air. His lunch felt like it would spring onto his desk like a frog. He was feeling light-headed when Allie suddenly spoke.

"I'd be happy to help Alex, Ms. Newton. I could start today."

He had to be daydreaming. He cleared his throat. "That'd be, uh, uh, great." Fantastic was more like it!

After class Alex thanked Robin and told her she was a real friend. There it was again. She was a friend, nothing more. Alex slapped her on the back and left. She watched him disappear in the crowd.

Before meeting with Allie that afternoon, Alex went to the restroom, wet his hair to punk it a little, popped a peppermint into his mouth, and rushed to the library.

"I wasn't sure if you could make it, what with football practice and all," Allie said when she saw him.

If she only knew—a band of marauding pirates couldn't keep him away. "Coach doesn't mind if we miss for academic reasons." Alex fished out a pencil. "Want me to get my book out too?"

"We can share mine."

He scooted his chair closer and sat down. She touched the back of his hand when she slid the book between them and his heart felt like it would do a half gainer out of his chest.

"What was it you were having trouble with?"

His thoughts ran like a mouse through a maze. He had to think of something. "Oh, uh—why don't we work on what we had in class today?"

She thumbed to page 192—Percentages. She began to explain the process, which he knew, but her voice was like music to his ears. He sighed. She smelled like roses. This was heaven, and she was an angel.

While Alex swooned at Bridgeport School, Frank Cooper sat in his home scheming about how he could get the name and address of the kid who owned the bike. When he formulated his plan, he dug out his little black address book, looked up a number and placed a call to the Kirk County Police Department. A perky voice answered.

"Records, Bonnie speaking."

Just hearing her voice made him feel queasy.

"Hi Bon, how's it going?" He forced himself to sound friendly. She wasn't exactly a dream girl, but she was his contact inside the police department.

"Why, you old devil you. Where've you been Frankie? I haven't heard from you in a coon's age. And what about that dinner you promised?"

"Now, Sweet Ca-a-akes. That's one of the reasons I called. Is tonight okay?"

Bonnie's head felt woozy. What luck. She'd been down on herself all morning about her weight and for eating those four doughnuts. Now this. You never know.

"Why, I'd love to Frankie."

"'Bout seven? How 'bout that little restaurant down by the river? You know, the boat with the good seafood."

"Ohhh, I love to eat there. And it's so romantic."

He almost choked. The woman could eat her way across the country. Too bad for her it wasn't an Olympic event. She'd win a gold medal.

"Sounds good," he said, burping quietly. "Oh—and—uh, I need a little favor, Bon. Do you think you could help me out?"

The phone went silent. He'd have to play this just right.

"It's nothing really. I know this guy who found a kid's bike and I told him he should return it." He forced a meek laugh. "You know me, Bon. I'd hate to see a kid lose her bike. I had one stolen when I was a little shaver and remember how upset I was. So, I just wanted the kid's name and address to tell him where to return it."

All he could hear on the other end was a fax machine running. He worried she might hang up. "So, what do you think, Bon? I've got the police I.D. number right here."

Bonnie's pencil broke as she jabbed it onto the tablet of paper on her desk. So that's what he wanted. But, Ol' Frankie was such a smooth talker she couldn't resist. And the thought of a date *and* a shrimp dinner—

"Ohhh, why not. It'll help the little kid. You were always such a big sweetie, Frankie. But you know that, don't ya?" She chuckled. "You say it's a girl's bike?"

He froze. It was a boy's bike. He slipped up, but did some quick thinking. "Don't really know. Could be either because I haven't seen it. He just told me he found one." He gave her the I.D. number before she could change her mind and she told him to hold on while she looked it up. This little bit of information was going to cost him big. She always drank too much and ordered the most expensive food. And, worst of all, when the evening was over she'd want to kiss him. But he would suffer through it. He would do anything if it would keep him out of jail.

She came back on the line. "Okay, here it is. Kid's name is Robin Beekler. That's B E E K L E R. Lives at 5419 Maple Road in Bridgeport. Blue Murray. Says here Robin is a girl, but she has a boy's bike."

"You don't know how much I appreciate this, Bon. Oh, by the way, let's just meet at the restaurant. I've got a meeting at seven and I don't want to keep a sweet thing like you waiting." She agreed and hung up.

Cooper leaned back in his chair to look at the paper in his hand. "Okay Miss Beekler," he said, "let's find out what you look like up close."

Cooper drove to the Bridgeport Library where they kept all the Bridgeport school yearbooks. He located last year's book and took it to a table hidden in the stacks. He quickly flipped through the pages for the B's for each grade and ran his finger down a page till he found it. Beekler, Robin.

She wore those same red tortoise shell glasses Buster had in his truck. A smart-looking kid with thick braids hanging over her shoulders. Looked like a decent kid. Too bad.

153

He peered around the bookshelves to see what the librarian was doing. She was busy checking out books to an older couple, so he quietly tore out the page with Robin's picture. He returned the book to the librarian, thanked her, and hurried outside to the black Chevy Blazer he had bought from a friend. The dark blue Buick he used to have was now out of the picture, since he abandoned it in the next county and reported it stolen.

While he waited at a stoplight, he pulled out Robin's picture to study it. He fixed her image in his mind. Everything, down to her pixie nose and the mole on the lower left side of her jaw. He tucked the picture into the inside pocket of his jacket when the traffic light turned green. He stomped the gas pedal. He was ready to make his next move and get a better look at Robin Beekler.

What Are Friends For?

❋ ❋ ❋ ❋ ❋ ❋

Kota called Dr. McKracken at the County Health Office and asked about the results of the soil samples from the cornfield. McKracken had no idea what he was talking about. Kota explained what had happened. McKracken told him he would send someone out immediately to get samples. He also gave Kota his word that he would call as soon as possible with the results. That afternoon Kota received the call.

"It's bad, Kota," McKracken began, "it's PERC, a toxic liquid used in the dry cleaning industry. It's also used by automobile parts manufacturers to clean metal so rubber can effectively adhere to it. There are strict government guidelines for its disposal. Unfortunately, some people dump the stuff wherever they can and falsify the disposal records. Then they pocket the money it would have taken to dispose of it according to federal guidelines. A black market has built up around dumping the stuff."

McKracken cleared his throat and went on, "After lunch

155

I rode out to Seth Dyer's field where the sample was taken and the smell alone told me it was PERC. I'm afraid we're going to have to destroy all the crops out there. They're probably all contaminated. And the land will have to undergo an entire reclamation process that'll take years. You said a girl saw a tanker truck out there late Friday night?"

"Yes. She's a friend of my grandson. The men chased her when they discovered she was there."

"Well, if she saw a tanker truck out there, it was dumping PERC, you can bet on that. It's a wonder she didn't get killed. There's a lot of money in that business and prison time if they're caught. I'd make sure her parents keep her real close to home. These kinds of scumbags don't fool around. They don't want a witness running around that could I.D. them."

"I'm driving her to school every morning and the police are patrolling her neighborhood in the afternoons. But Doc, you know how the Bridgeport police force is. They're short-staffed and have their own priorities."

"You see what those guys did with the soil sample," McKracken said, "clean forgot about it, I assume. Sloppy police work. According to the readings, the concentration levels were off the chart, so these criminals must have been doing this for some time. I sure hope no one's eaten that corn. I'll have to look into that. If we're lucky, they just started dumping this growing season and are long gone by now. Let's hope so anyway."

"Does Sheriff Newby know the results yet?" Kota asked.

"Sure. I called him myself. I also asked him why I hadn't gotten the sample. He said the deputy had been busy and hadn't been able to drop it off yet."

"Too busy?"

"Right."

"Did the sheriff say he'd continue the investigation?"

"If he wants to keep his job, he will," McKracken said.

After Kota hung up, he contemplated the dreadful results. The land couldn't be replanted for years. He leaned back in the chair and thought of Seth and how upset his friend would have been. He could easily imagine the scenario. Seth had discovered what they were doing and tried to stop them. Considering his age and health, he wouldn't have stood a chance against the men, however many there were. Now everyone had lost. Seth, the people who could have eaten the food, the stores that could have sold it, and Robin. She was a witness, a loose end the men would not forget. They would come for her, and possibly Alex. He was sure of it.

At least now the police would know she was telling the truth. Now they would be more serious about protecting her and searching for the men. The question remaining was whether the small police department could handle it.

Kota thought of the vision he'd had a few nights earlier. The one he hadn't mentioned to anyone. The one about fire, water, and death. His body suddenly felt old and tired. He ran a glass of water at the sink and noticed his hand trembled. Sometimes knowing, always knowing, took its toll. He massaged his hand and looked at the picture under his refrigerator magnet—a photo of Alex, Marc, and Robin taken at an amusement park. In the background was a roller coaster. In his mind's eye, he saw a black rose appear and hover above their images. The sign. Someone was going to die. He placed the glass in the sink and walked outside to his meditation garden. When his feet touched earth, another image flashed in his mind. A yellow car speeding toward a railroad crossing while the crossarms were dropping. He rubbed his forehead as hard as he could, but there was no way it would erase the visions he'd seen the last few days and what he knew would come to pass. Amid the rocks, plants, and Indian treasures, he dropped to his knees and lifted his arms to heaven.

Tuesday afternoon Robin rode the bus home while Marc and Alex stayed after school for practice. When the bus driver got to her stop at the corner of Maple and Pike, Robin hopped down the steps and swung her book bag over her shoulder. She looked both ways while crossing the street in front of the bus. When she cleared Pike Road and started down Maple, she kicked a rock along ahead of her. She didn't like the days when Marc and Alex weren't on the school bus, nor the days when her mother worked late. Down the street, she saw a squad car pulling off Pike onto Maple Street and felt a lot better.

The bus driver, Mr. Thompson, did not drive off right away. Instead, he waited for the black SUV parked at the edge of the road ahead of him, unsure whether the driver intended to pull out or not. The man finally stuck his arm out the window and waved for the bus to go around.

Mr. Thompson slowly pulled around him, but did look down at the car to see what the man was doing. The man, wearing a green ball cap, was looking at some papers resting on his steering wheel. Lost—probably. Mr. Thompson dismissed it and drove around the SUV.

In his rear view mirror, Frank Cooper watched Robin Beekler wave to the deputy cruising by. She crossed her front yard, unlocked the door, and walked in. *No one to meet her? She was alone.*

He watched the squad car pull into a driveway and turn around. As the officer accelerated, he tipped his hat towards the girl standing in her doorway and drove off. Cooper checked his watch—3:45. He eased the SUV onto the road and headed the opposite way from the squad car. In his side view mirror, he watched it drive away and figured the cop never saw him. He waited for the officer to turn toward town and that's exactly what he did. He smiled, tossing the cap onto the passenger's seat. This operation was going to be as easy as taking candy from a baby.

Who's Watching Robin?

✳ ✳ ✳ ✳ ✳ ✳

Late that afternoon, Alex sat at his desk, chin propped on his hand, staring into space. *Allie. Beautiful Allie.* Things couldn't have worked out any better. He thought of when he sat next to her in the library and had savored every moment. Touching her hand when he reached for the pencil. Feeling her arm against his. He pictured them becoming Homecoming King and Queen in their senior year and holding hands while riding in the back of a convertible. He thought of them graduating, getting married—married? He straightened in his seat.

Kota appeared at the bedroom doorway, saw the stack of CD's on the desk and the unpacked book bag on the chair.

"*Iho*, I thought you were doing your homework."

"I will. I was just doing some thinking." He didn't want to tell him it was about Allie. "Want something, Grandpa?"

"Thought you'd want to know I'm about to call Sonny Dyer up in Madison."

"Seth's son? You're calling him?"

160

Kota nodded.

"You bet I'm interested." Alex jumped out of the chair.

"Here, use my phone."

Kota looked at the messy desk. "I'll call from the kitchen."

While Kota flipped through his address book, he said, "Do you remember what I taught you about tracking and marking trails?"

"Yes sir. What does that have to do with Sonny Dyer?"

"Nothing," Kota said. "It was just on my mind today. You kids must watch out for one another till these men are caught. If something happens, use those skills I taught you. Understand?"

"Yes, *Tunkašila*—Grandpa. Don't worry. I'll remember if the time ever comes."

"Good. You and Marc came home today with Mr. Corby?"

Alex nodded.

"And dropped Robin off?"

Alex was dumfounded. He hadn't once thought about Robin being alone. Sitting close to Allie had vaporized his brain.

"I, uh, don't know." He felt horrible. "I'll call her now."

"She's okay, Alex. I already checked on her. But this cannot happen again. You must stick together at all times. I cannot tell you how critical that is."

"I know, Grandpa. I know. I just forgot today. I won't forget again. I promise."

His grandfather looked worried. Alex got an uneasy feeling. "Is there something I should know? Did something happen?"

Kota told him about the soil sample from Seth's cornfield.

"They're going to destroy Seth's crops? But that's a lot of corn. And what about the artifacts?"

"The land will have to be reclaimed, and those men will pay for what they did. If not in this life, *Wakan Tanka* will make them account for everything in another."

"I've got to tell Marc and Robin," he said.

"First let's call Sonny. It will just take a few minutes."

Kota called Sonny Dyer in Madison, Indiana, while Alex leaned close to listen.

"Sonny? This is Kota Sanders, your father's neighbor."

"And friend," Alex heard Sonny say. His voice sounded nice. That confused him because he had him pegged as the murderer and murderers weren't supposed to be nice.

"Thank you," Kota said. "I can't tell you how sorry I am about your father's death. He was one of the finest men I've ever known. I know you miss him. Is there anything I can do for you?"

"Just being such a good friend to my father for all these years is more than enough. He spoke of you often. Always with great respect."

"I hope you're doing okay," Kota said.

"Yes, considering the circumstances. You know, Kota, I didn't see him much in the last few years, what with the distance and my job. But I sure do miss him and I regret not seeing him more often." His voice broke.

"I'm sorry. You can be proud that he was such an honorable man. My people would call him *Wicaśa Okinihan*—honorable and respected."

Sonny repeated it. "Thanks, Kota. That would have meant a lot to Dad."

"Another reason I called is Rags, your dad's dog. I was afraid you might be worried about him. I wanted you to know I have him."

"Ah, thank goodness, Kota. I went over Saturday and looked but couldn't find him anywhere."

"I'm sorry. I should have called you sooner, but a lot's been going on here." He filled Sonny in on what had happened with Seth and his land.

Sonny was shocked.

"I'll let you know what happens. And before I forget, what do you want me to do about Rags?"

Alex tensed.

"I'll have to figure that one out," Sonny said.

"I'll keep him as long as you want. He has good energy and it is an honor to care for him."

"Thank you, Kota. I'll let you know when I can pick him up."

"Take your time. Whenever you're ready for him, let me know. Oh, I have one other question. Have you decided what you're going to do with the farm?"

Alex pressed closer.

"I'm not sure. Especially with all this PERC stuff you're talking about. It's been great farmland but it won't be now, at least for a while. Oh Lord, Dad loved that land. All this contamination business would have broken his heart. I'll have to think this through and let you know what I decide."

"That land was Seth's life."

And death, Alex thought.

"I'll probably keep the wildlife preserve as it is—dedicate it to him and the animals. And by the way, Kota, Dad left you a tract of land—the section adjoining your property."

Kota paused. "I'm honored. And I'll see that the land is honored. You are a good son. You serve your father's heart. I know he is proud. There should be no regrets."

Kota hung up the phone and turned to Alex. "Well, still think he's the murderer?"

Alex shrugged. "No, Grandpa. He seemed really nice, just like Seth."

"He is, Alex. And he's trying to do the right thing for the land. Apparently the contamination is a complete surprise to him, too."

Alex got Marc and Robin on a three-way call and told them about the contamination and Sonny Dyer's plans for the land. He told them he didn't think Sonny was their man. They would have to find another suspect. Robin said she wasn't so sure.

The next afternoon, Frank Cooper followed the school bus at a safe distance. He saw the squad car again and watched Robin get off the bus. He noted the time. Once again, 3:45. Mornings were completely out because that mountain of an Indian picked up the kids like clockwork. Buster had discovered that when he watched the houses from the woods.

Buster had also found a new dump site. He might not be as stupid as Cooper thought. From the information they gathered, it looked as though the afternoon would be the best time to strike. He would simply create a diversion for the police, then lure the girl into the car and do away with her.

Things were getting complicated, but he'd been through worse. He touched the scar on his face. Much worse. But it would all be over soon. He'd have $200,000 in his pocket, Buster and the kid would be history, and he'd be on his way to Costa Rica.

The next morning, when Kota picked up the kids, they talked non-stop about the contamination and Seth's land until Robin changed the subject.

"How'd the tutoring go, Alex?"

"Great! There's no other way to describe it."

"Tutoring?" Kota said. "You didn't mention you needed tutoring."

Marc laughed. "He doesn't. He just likes the tutor."

Alex felt his face go hot. "She's beautiful, Grandpa."

Kota nodded. "Ah, I understand."

Marc looked at him. "By the way, Alex, I heard Jed got really mad when he found out about Allie tutoring you. So watch your back."

"I figured something was up," Alex said. "When he walked by me in the locker room yesterday, he bumped my shoulder."

"You didn't tell me that!" Robin said. "What'd you do?"

"What could I do? He can clean my clock anytime he wants, so I pretended it was an accident. I was just glad Allie wasn't around to see it." He fidgeted with the strap on his book bag. "He's been pretty nasty in practice, too."

"If you want, I can walk with you between classes," Marc told him. "Two's better than one, and Jed knows I won't stand by and do nothing."

"Pick your battles," Kota told them. "Walk away from unimportant things, and the things that are important, well—you stand up for those. The hard part is staying calm enough to recognize the difference. And keep in mind that school is not a place for fighting. It's a place of learning. It's more important to keep your eyes on your goals than on the bumps in the road."

The old rusty truck rumbled over a pothole. They bounced on the seat.

Alex picked his books up from the floor. "You need to keep your eyes on the road, Grandpa."

"The tough part," Robin added, "is when the potholes get so big they swallow you up."

A Pint-Sized Witness

✳ ✳ ✳ ✳ ✳ ✳

At football practice on Thursday, Marc and Alex got their clocks not only cleaned, but shined in the process. But so did Jed and his friend Mike. It started when Jed and Mike tackled Alex harder than necessary. For Alex, that was the final straw. He got up, lunged head first at Jed, ramming him in the stomach and knocking him backwards onto the ground. The next thing Alex knew, the whole team piled on. Every boy, it seemed, wanted a piece of Jed Howard and on that Thursday, they got it. Even the coach took his time breaking up the fight. In the final analysis, Alex was sore, but it was a small price to pay for his reputation and setting things straight.

While Marc and Alex were at practice, Frank Cooper drove a 'borrowed' blue jeep towards the corner of Pike and Maple, wearing sunglasses and a ball cap pulled low on his forehead. He checked his watch: 3:45 p.m. Up ahead, he saw the school bus roll to a stop. His timing was perfect. He pulled up behind the bus to wait and watch when he noticed the squad car waiting on Robin's street. That was the fourth consecutive day. He was running out of time and fumed as Robin crossed the road and waved at the policeman in the squad car.

He clenched his teeth as he thought about the radio report saying the police had an eyewitness and were looking for two men in connection with the farmer's killing. The report also mentioned the PERC being dumped—and the kid could connect everything back to them. She had to be eliminated.

And there she was—a pint-sized witness—just yards from him. He wanted to gun the engine, mow her down like a weed and outrun the cops. But that was too risky. He would have to wait till tomorrow. Fridays were hectic days for the police. Especially if there were emergency calls. He would see to it that those calls were at 3:40 and for the other side of town.

That evening, Frank Cooper drove to Dixie's for another meeting with Buster. To his surprise, Buster was already there, waiting in the back booth. Frank caught Julie's attention, ordered a cup of coffee, and joined him.

"Want another cup?" Cooper asked, pointing to Buster's nearly empty one.

"No, just want to know the plan."

Frank folded his arms and leaned on the tabletop. "Let's take care of loose ends first. Did you take care of the glasses?"

Buster fished through the pockets of his jacket, then slapped the red horn-rimmed glasses on the table in front of Frank.

"What do you think you're doing?" Frank's voice sounded frantic.

"My truck was misfiring so I had to get it tuned up. I didn't want to leave the glasses in it, like you said, so I took 'em out. Haven't had a chance to hide 'em. You do it."

Before Cooper could reach for the glasses, Julie appeared and set down the steaming cup of coffee. "Whoa! I almost put your coffee on those." She started to slide them over, but instead picked them up. "These are kid's glasses, aren't they?"

Cooper wanted to snatch them, but restrained himself.

"You know my husband's niece has a pair of glasses just like these. Same color, same style, same company. And look at that." She pointed to the glued spot on the bridge. "Hers broke too, but I think it was a little farther over. Humph, they'll probably have a recall on them. You know they make millions of these." She looked at him and asked, "You have kids?"

Both men sipped their coffee. Cooper did some fast thinking and said, "Buster found them on the road in

Connersville and asked me to drop them by the Lion's Club. You know how they recycle frames for kids who can't afford new ones."

"Yeah. There's a box in my doctor's office where people can leave them. Who knows, maybe they can match up the kid with the glasses." She set them back on the table, took their order, and left for the kitchen.

Cooper grabbed the glasses, stuffed them into his shirt pocket, and leaned across the table. "What did I tell you?"

Buster wiped sweat from his face with a paper napkin.

For the next hour and a half Cooper went over and over their plan for Friday night. Buster would pick up the next load and dump it at the new location while Cooper would take care of the Beekler kid. He'd pick her up, blindfold her, and hold her till the last dump was finished tomorrow night. After that, he'd drive her twenty miles from Bridgeport and release her at a rest stop. He'd pick up the money and meet Buster and they'd go their separate ways.

The plan sounded great to Buster. They would each get their split and the kid wouldn't get hurt. They went over the plan one final time and agreed not to communicate again until they met late Friday night.

Cooper paid Julie and they started for the door. On their way out a young man wearing a plaid shirt walked in and stopped, blocking the doorway. Cooper waited for him to step aside when the guy yelled, "Julie. Julie Beekler! I haven't seen you since high school. You still going to college somewhere?"

Cooper froze. *Beekler? Her niece had glasses like these?* He watched Julie and the guy head for a table. *She's the kid's aunt! Now she's seen the glasses—seen them with the glasses.*

"Did you hear that?" Cooper said in a hushed voice. "Julie's last name is Beekler. She's the kid's aunt! And you practically waved the glasses in her face."

"Cool down, Coop. You heard her. She doesn't think they're hers. Said there were millions of them. Get a grip, for Pete's sake. I've never seen you like this."

Cooper ran his fingers through his hair. Wasn't much they could do about it now. "Yeah. Guess you're right. She didn't seem to think anymore about it. Besides, it'll all be over tomorrow night." He opened the door and started for his car, but stopped when he remembered about Stan. "Hey, Buster."

Buster looked over his shoulder as he reached his rusted green station wagon.

"You've got it all set up with Stan, right?"

"You don't trust me with nothing, do ya?" Buster snapped. "It's done. He's as ready as we are to get this thing over."

Cooper climbed into his SUV and slammed the door. As he drove home, he considered what happened at Dixie's. Things could crash like a house of cards. Fortunately, it would all be over tomorrow.

He went over his plan—not the one he discussed with Buster, but the real one. The one where he ends up with all the money and no loose ends. After the last delivery, he'd take care of Buster. Then he'd take I-65 south to Nashville where he'd catch a 6:00 a.m. flight. With $200,000, he could live like a king in Costa Rica.

He looked up at the sky as he drove along the winding rural road. It was beautiful, dark and clear, dotted with stars that twinkled like diamonds. He drew in a breath of night air and wondered if they were even brighter in Costa Rica.

Two and Two Make Four
✶ ✶ ✶ ✶ ✶ ✶

Julie Beekler dressed for art class Friday morning while her husband Bob called Robin's house to see how she was doing. It was something he did once a week even though Robin's mother was divorced from his brother and had remarried.

Julie listened while she put on makeup.

"Hi Mary, Bob here. How's Robin? How's the bike holding up?"

In the mirror, Julie saw Bob's smile fade.

"The glasses too? Poor kid. Hope Stanley didn't give her a hard time about it."

"Glasses?" Julie said half to herself and turned, giving him her full attention.

"Two men?" he said.

Julie put down the tube of mascara.

"The police are watching the house, aren't they? Poor kid must be scared to death. I'll stop by later this afternoon

174

when she gets home from school. Oh, no problem. Call if you need anything."

Julie grabbed his arm as soon as he pushed the OFF button on his cell phone. "What's all this about the glasses and two men?" she asked, starting to nibble her thumbnail.

He stared at her. "What is it, honey? You're white as your nightgown."

"Robin's glasses are red tortoise shell—right? And they're glued somewhere on the bridge?"

"Yeah."

Julie sank onto the bed next to him.

"You know something, don't you?"

"Oh, Bob. Last night, at Dixie's, two men had a pair of glasses like Robin's."

He shrugged, "So?"

"These guys have been in several times. But last night they had a pair of kid's glasses—just like Robin's. I even mentioned that when I asked whose they were."

"What'd they say?"

"That someone had asked them to drop them off at the Lion's Club." She wrung her hands. "Bob, I see those glasses all over the place. If I'd only known Robin's were missing I might've put two and two together." She looked at him. "She must be in danger if the police are watching her house."

"Yeah, apparently she's the only person who can identify them."

"This thing with the glasses is just too much of a coincidence," Julie insisted. "I mean, Robin loses her glasses and her bicycle, and two men chase her. Then two men come into Dixie's and lay identical glasses on the table while they talk. And I'm telling you, Bob, they got awfully nervous when I picked up those glasses and asked about them. One even broke out in a sweat."

"You said they'd been in there a few times?"

"Yes, and they always seem to be, I don't know, scheming and looking over their shoulders. They're real creeps if you ask me, especially the one with the long scar on his face." She chewed her nail till Bob pulled it away from her mouth. "Bob, if the police are watching her house, they must think the men know her name and address. But how?"

He smacked his head with his hand. "The bike! I insisted she get the bike I.D.'d in case it ever got lost or stolen. Oh, great. If those men have any contacts inside the police department, they can get that information."

Julie jumped up.

"What is it?"

"If they know her name is Beekler, they know I'm related to her."

"No, honey, remember your name tag just has 'Julie' on it."

"I'm telling you, they know my last name. Listen. When they were leaving Dixie's last night Phil Mixson came in and called out my name—my whole name. Then the guy with the scar turned and stared at me. I'll never forget that look." She rubbed her arms. "I'm telling you Bob. He's creepy and dark-looking like some kind of, I don't know, gangster or pirate, or something."

He picked up the phone and dialed the police. "You said they'd been in a couple of times. Did you ever catch their names?"

"Frank and Buster. But that's all I know."

"Can you identify them?"

"Oh yeah, with that scar, there's no mistaking Frank. He's tall with black, receding hair and is real moody and obsessive. A real germ freak. He's always rearranging his silverware, wiping it off, or asking for new ones."

Bob got a detective on the line and handed Julie the phone. She explained everything and agreed to go to the police station immediately to look through some mug shots. If the men's pictures weren't in the file, the artist would make composite drawings from her descriptions. Julie agreed, but the trip was bad timing. She had an art history exam in one hour, but Robin's life was far more important than a college course.

Julie quickly changed and headed out the door to her little yellow car. She backed out of the drive, shoved the gear into first, and gunned the engine. She raced towards the first intersection as the light turned yellow. She accelerated to get through it. Every second counted now. She geared down to second and took the next corner as fast as she dared. The tires squealed but she held the steering wheel steady and shifted into third, then fourth. She had to hurry so the police could find the men before they got to Robin.

She raced down Plymouth Street and, through her open window, heard a train whistle blow. Ahead at the crossing, the railroad lights began to flash. She couldn't believe her luck. It was the 8:10 freight train, and it was as long as the city was wide. She had to beat the cross arms.

She stomped her foot on the gas pedal, gripped the steering wheel, and aimed for the center of the road. The speedometer hit sixty. The cross arms were about fifty feet away and beginning to drop. She bit her lip and braced herself as she neared the crossing.

The ends of the railroad cross arms passed one another on the downward arc. Julie swerved hard to the left, missing the first one. The raised steel tracks caused the car to bounce over the rails and the steering wheel to jerk violently, making a sound like a jackhammer. The tires hit so hard, her teeth clicked together in double bumps. She jerked the wheel back to the right to skirt the second arm that came within inches of her window. Had she been in Bob's SUV, the arm would have smashed the hood. The car skidded sideways, hit a patch of gravel, and spun twice before hitting the curb on the opposite side of the road. It teetered to a stop and the engine died. Gray road dust flurried around the car like a fog. She dropped her head against the steering wheel as a hubcap rolled down the street, toppled and drum-rolled to a spinning stop. The train reached the crossing with a roar that ripped through her car. The whistle blasted, making her nearly jump out of her skin.

"Stupid, stupid, stupid," she muttered, thumping her head on the steering wheel. "Unbelievably stupid."

An approaching driver honked the horn because she was stopped on the wrong side of the street and facing him. With a shaky foot, she depressed the clutch, started the engine, and shifted into first. Her entire body trembled. She pulled onto the right side of the road, shifted into second, and noticed a speed sign marked thirty-five miles per hour. She shifted into third and held the speedometer at exactly thirty-five all the way to the station.

Robin was quiet on the ride to school that morning. When Alex asked if she was okay, she said her stepfather had been in a really bad mood. That wasn't anything unusual, but something else bothered her. She said she'd had an uneasy feeling all morning. Marc pointed out that it was Friday the 13th.

She sneered. "It's a day like any other day. And I'm not superstitious, except—"

Marc looked at her. "Except what?"

"That weird moon. I couldn't sleep for thinking about it."

"I heard about that," Alex said. "It was upside-down."

"Yeah. Like a frown in the sky." She formed a curve with her thumb and forefinger. "It was creepy, like something in a horror movie."

"*Hanhepi wi*—the moon," Kota said, "gives us light in the midst of darkness."

Robin mouthed the Indian words silently. "Well, I did some research on this particular *hanhepi wi* on the internet yesterday. And what I found out is really freaky. According to this one site, some people think the moon is an omen or a warning. It said that when an upside-down moon appears, ghosts of old pirates come back and take human form."

"Pirates?" Alex said, looking at her.

"That's right," Kota said. "Years ago, they attacked boats on the Ohio River and retreated to this area to hide in the hills where no one could find them. The pirates had no respect for people or the land and treated both cruelly. They were people who traveled the Black Road, similar to the men who ordered the mass slaughter of hundreds of thousands of buffalo to kill the Lakota's lifeline of food. Aside from hunting parties, they used trains with dozens of men on each side of passenger cars shooting *Tatanka*, buffalo, as they went. You can imagine the carnage. And the waste. When just one *Tatanka* provided my people with much food, clothing, tools, and more. The buffalo and Lakota barely survived."

"That's horrible," Robin said, wiping her eyes. "They were Prairie Pirates."

"I thought I saw a Pirate in the cornfield the day Robin and I found Seth's body," Alex said, "but the whole thing was quick as a flash. I just thought it was my imagination."

"Probably was," Kota said, rubbing his temple.

Alex asked, "What did the article say these ghosts would do?"

"Plunder, rob, and murder."

"Seth?" Marc said.

Robin looked out the window.

Alex swallowed. "I had trouble sleeping too. I kept dreaming, but I don't know why or what happened because I kept waking up every time the dream got to a black car."

Kota also had a bad feeling as he stared at the road. The headache he'd had all morning was worse. And he knew why: with his sixth sense, headaches were like clouds before a storm. But he couldn't mention that to the kids. Pirates and ghosts—their imaginations were already working overtime. The headache wouldn't go away until he knew the kids were out of harm's way. What he really wanted to do was drive the kids to his house in the woods and keep them there till the killers were caught. But they had to go to school. They'd be safe, there. The problem was after school.

"How about having a 3-M Night at my house tonight? You can all sleep in sleeping bags on the floor in front of the fireplace. Kind of a camp-out or a camp in, I suppose."

They jumped at the idea. They loved Kota's place. It was secluded and filled with Indian artifacts.

"Good," Kota said. "Robin, the patrol car will be waiting for you when you get off the bus today. Check with your parents and let me know. I will come get you around six. Do not walk or ride anywhere. The same goes for you boys. Do you understand?"

Within minutes, Kota dropped the three kids at school and watched them enter the building. He pulled away from the curb and headed to the grocery to get supplies for the lodge. Halfway there, the skin on the back of his neck felt as though bees were swarming inside it. It was a message he understood all too well—something bad was coming.

Detective Steve Owens set a steaming cup of coffee next to Julie as she sketched the faces of the two men. She finished and handed him the sketchpad. He couldn't believe she remembered so many details.

"That's a sparkler," she said, pointing to the diamond earring in Frank's ear. "Over three karats." She tilted her head, studied the picture, then rubbed some of the charcoal penciling off the edge of the beard. "It's ironic, really."

"What's that?" the Detective asked.

"I've had the urge to draw this character since the first time I saw him at Dixie's. There was something about the way his beard framed his face, and those dark eyes that made me want to capture him on paper."

"Even if he shaved the beard and stashed the earring, that scar and those eyes would nail him," Detective Owens noticed.

"He's vain and very particular about his looks. I think he grew the beard to hide the scar, but the hair didn't fill in over the scar tissue. Looks like he grew it long enough to comb it over."

Owens laid down the picture of Frank and looked at her sketch of Buster.

"Buster's been coming into Dixie's for some time," Julie said. "I think he works at the tire factory. A driver, possibly, but I'm not sure. Should be easy to check since you have a first name and picture."

"You've made our work a lot easier, Mrs. Beekler. We sure do appreciate it." He blew on his hot coffee, then sipped. "It's a lucky break for us, and for your niece, that you're an artist. I'll get some people out to the factory right away to check out this guy." He glanced at his watch. "The plant's still open but some of the drivers operate on a contract basis and keep their own hours. Buster may not be there now, but we'll nab him when he turns up or find him wherever he is."

Julie drank the rest of her coffee. "If you have anymore questions, you know how to reach me." She got up to go, but stopped in the doorway. "Detective, please find these guys before they get to Robin. She's the sweetest kid in the world and I'd hate for anything to happen to her."

Owens patted her arm and said, "I promise you, Mrs. Beekler, we'll do everything in our power to catch these guys before they hurt anyone else. I'll run the pictures through the system right now." He held up Frank's picture. "With a face like that he's got to have a rap sheet. I'll call Bob the minute we know something." She started to leave when he added, "And, Mrs. Beekler, you be careful, too."

The school day started with the best announcement a student could hear: second period was being shortened to accommodate an assembly. On top of that, Alex got an "A" on a literature test. Before he knew it, it was noon and he was headed for the lunchroom. He felt so upbeat, he decided to make the big move and sit by Allie.

He left the lunch line with an extra cookie and found her sitting four tables away with an empty chair next to her. She looked his way and his breath caught in his throat. It was the critical moment. *Should he nod and sit somewhere else or walk right up and plop down his tray?* He was about to make this move when he heard the lunch lady call him back. He couldn't believe the bad timing. Someone would take the seat. When he reached the register, she held up his fifty cents change. He stuffed it into his pocket, turned, and saw

Allie signaling him to join her. Two hundred kids in the cafetorium became a blur as he glided towards her.

Robin left the lunch line and glanced around the cafetorium for Alex who had been several people ahead of her. Then she saw him sitting near the center with Allie. Her tray and mood lowered by degrees and she shuffled to an empty table in the back.

Alex sat down and laid the snickerdoodle cookie on Allie's tray. Her smile broadened—till Marc appeared across the table and slapped down his tray. His rear end couldn't have warmed the seat before he asked Allie if she'd seen Jed lately. Alex choked. Milk dribbled out his nose and Allie had to slap him on the back.

When he stopped coughing, she stabbed her plastic fork into her mystery casserole, making both the fork and the food wobble. "Don't ever mention his name around me."

Alex couldn't believe his ears as he wiped his face with his napkin.

Allie went on, "He trails me like Freddy Krueger and then talks my ears off. I could just freak out and die. Do me a favor—if you see him coming, warn me so I can duck out!"

"Sure. As long as you do the same for us." Marc winked at Alex. "I think I'll go find the Robster now. She's probably eating by herself somewhere. Catch ya later, dude, Allie." He popped a french fry into his mouth and stood to look for Robin. When he spotted her, he headed across the room.

Alex looked into Allie's blue eyes as she took a dainty bite of the casserole. She did it so perfectly, he could imagine her in a commercial eating something really exotic, like nachos and dip, or lasagna.

One table over, airborne, ketchuped fries struck Frankie Smith's face and slid down the inside of his shirt. A fight ensued. Chairs banged against tables and fell onto the floor. French fries sailed past Alex. Kids all over the cafetorium abandoned their lunches and scampered to join the excitement.

In the midst of the mayhem, Alex reached under the table. When their fingers touched, she squeezed his hand. His heart swelled in his chest and despite the fighting and screaming all around, he was in heaven.

Marc and Robin watched Sam Jenkins disappear under the table as Frankie dove for him. Students flocked to the area like flies to a cow patty to watch the fight. Mr. Michaels shoved his way to the middle, lifted the two boys off the floor, ordered everyone back to their seats, and hauled the troublemakers off to the principal's office.

Marc shook his head. "Jenkins is such a fool. Toss fries at somebody like Frankie and it's lights out, plus detention."

"You came awfully close to getting detention when you helped me with Brad. I really appreciated it, Marc, but I sure hated you getting in trouble over it."

"That's what friends are for, Robster. Besides, he's a

creep and he had it coming. I oughta thank you for giving me the opportunity. So, tell me why you're sitting back here?"

She looked towards Alex, then down at her tray. "I just didn't feel like I was good company today. I guess things just seem weird right now."

"Alex, you mean?"

"Yeah, he's—different," she said.

"Different isn't the word for it. Look at him."

Robin looked, again. Alex was staring at Allie.

"He's pathetic," Marc said. "But he'll be back to his old self in another week when the Allie thing cools off. You'll see."

When the final bell rang, Alex joined the stampede that was more like a prison break. It had been an amazing day. He leapt up the bus steps, floated to his seat, and plopped down. When he looked through the window, he saw a line of stormy dark clouds moving in. He thought of the killers and his tingling excitement dwindled.

By the time the bus turned onto Pike Road, the sky was black. He heard the rumble of distant thunder and looked across the aisle at Robin. Her pencil tapped nervously on the seat in front of her.

She looked over at him. "I'm glad your grandpa is having us over because Mom and Stanley have been working late and I feel like a sitting duck when I'm at my house alone."

He leaned across the aisle, lowering his voice. "You know this morning when you said you had a weird feeling?"

She nodded.

"That's what I've been feeling since I got on the bus. Kind of like the air is charged with something."

The pudgy kid behind them started to hum the theme song from *The Twilight Zone*.

Alex shot him a dirty look. The kid shifted in his seat and a high-pitched ripping sound pierced the air. The kids nearby laughed and thrashed around in their seats till their nostrils filled with the scent of rotten eggs. Alex wanted to choke the brat but needed fresh air more, so he stood and let down the window.

When the smell dissipated, he leaned over the seat in front of him where Marc sat reading. He tapped him on the shoulder. "I hope we get home before the rain starts."

When the bus came to a stop at Maple and Pike, Robin hefted her book bag over her shoulder. "See you guys later." She walked down the aisle, hopped down the steps, and looked both ways as the bus pulled away. *Where was the police car?* She started to turn back to the bus, but it was already grinding into second gear. She dropped the book bag at her feet, and watched the bus bump down the street.

From his seat by the window Alex watched Robin stop at the corner and drop her bag. *What was she doing?* Robin waved frantically, but the driver didn't stop. She picked up her book bag, hitched it over her shoulder, and with her head down walked slowly toward her house.

Alex stared at the driver's back, unsure of what to do. The bus took the S-curve and from that angle he could see all the way down her street. And there, parked near her house, was a black SUV.

He jumped to his feet, hitting his head against the curve of the roof. He rubbed his head as he hit Marc on the shoulder. "We've got to get off the bus!"

Marc looked up from his book. "What are you talking about, man?"

"There's a black car back there. On Robin's street! Remember my dream? Robin's in trouble, I just know it!"

Alex started for the front, but the bus leaned into a turn and he had to hold onto the edge of a seat. Marc balanced both book bags over one arm and followed till he stopped to brace against another seat.

"Mr. Thompson!" Alex yelled. "We've got to get off the bus!" He stooped to see out the window and saw Robin walking toward the car.

"Stop the bus, Mr. Thompson!" he yelled, shaking the driver's shoulder.

"I can't stop the bus here, young man! Get back to your seat."

"We have to get off the bus. It's an emergency. Robin's in trouble back there."

"This isn't a designated stop. School rules. So sit down!"

Alex looked through the window again. Across the field, he saw a man get out of the car and walk towards Robin. The bus turned another curve and he lost sight of them.

Alex panicked. The only thing he could do now was yank the door lever and jump out. He held onto the seat and reached out for the lever when Marc called out, "I'm going to be sick! I've got to throw up!"

Mr. Thompson looked in the rear view mirror and saw Marc standing in the aisle with his hand over his mouth. He slammed on the brakes, causing Marc and Alex to nearly topple over. Mr. Thompson shoved the lever and yelled, "Get out, fast! Do it out there!"

Alex and Marc leapt down the steps and bolted toward Robin's house.

When Mr. Thompson saw Marc sprint down the road, he slid open his window and called out, "You boys are going to be in big trouble come Monday morning. I'm turning in a report on both of you."

That was the least of their worries. Marc caught up with Alex and tossed him his book bag. They ran as fast as they could carrying the bags, but still had a distance to go. It would take several minutes—several minutes that could make a difference in whether Robin lived—or died.

Before the bus appeared, Frank Cooper sat in his car watching black clouds gather. He willed the rain to hold off till he got the kid in the car. If it rained, she would run straight to her house and not stop. For his plan to work, he needed her to get close so he could get her into the car.

He cracked his knuckles and checked his watch for the millionth time. The schmutz should be there soon. In the minutes he waited, he reviewed everything he'd done to make sure he hadn't forgotten a thing. At 3:40 p.m. he disguised his voice and placed an emergency call to the police to report a break-in in progress on the other side of town. At 3:42 he placed another emergency call for a hit and run. This one was in a remote area of Bridgeport that was no where near Robin's street. He made both calls from his car parked on Ash Street. At 3:43 he drove to Maple and parked his car so it faced Pike Road rather than the cul-de-sac.

He wore a telephone company shirt and a ball cap with matching logos. Everything was set. He picked up the can of pop from the cup holder, took a drink, and tossed the aluminum can out the window. He picked up the clipboard and positioned the map at just the right angle across the seat. Everything was going perfectly, except for the weather. He should have considered a back-up plan.

He went over the plan one last time. He would stop the girl and ask where the Bradys lived. He would show her the work order he'd printed from his computer. It looked legit.

Robin wouldn't know where the Bradys lived because they were bogus. He would ask her to look at the map lying on the seat. While she looked at the map he'd pull out the chloroform, pop the top, and soak the cloth with it. Then he'd shove the cloth on her face and hold it there. In seconds she would be out. If she started to awaken, he would pull the car over and gag and tie her with the duct tape hidden under the seat. Then he'd take her to the woods near his cabin, shoot her, and let the animals take care of the rest. He'd wipe the prints off the car and ditch it.

The gun, complete with silencer, was under the seat next to the duct tape. What a plan! Neat and clean to the very end, when he'd collect the money and fly to Costa Rica. Unless it rains! He tried to think of something, when the yellow bus appeared at the end of the road and screeched to a stop. A sigh of relief crossed his lips.

He leaned forward over the steering wheel and watched the red-haired munchkin walk down the aisle of the bus. He checked the windshield. No drops, although the wind had picked up and the sky had blackened.

He watched her start across the street. It was her, alright. His heart began to pound with excitement till she stopped. *Why had she done that? What was wrong?* Then it hit him. The police car wasn't there. To his horror, she started waving her arms toward the bus.

He slammed his fist on the steering wheel. Fool! You

should have thought of that. Now, instead of a police car, she's looking at a strange man in a strange car. He had to do something fast or the kid would bolt. He quickly opened the door and stepped out.

Cooper was careful not to look Robin's way as she came down the street. Instead, he acted as though he was trying to find street numbers. He kept looking back at his papers and scratching the back of his neck.

Robin noticed the telephone insignia on his cap. "You lost, mister?"

He acted surprised. "Oh! You startled me," he said, placing his hand to his chest. "Yes, I am, as a matter of fact. I'm not familiar with this area. I normally work the Clarksville area, so I'm a little turned around."

Robin stared at his long scar and dark beard. He reminded her of a pirate, and there was something familiar about him.

Got to watch the voice, he thought, in case the kid recognizes it from that night in the cornfield. He shrugged his shoulders, softened his tone.

"I can't seem to find the address listed on this order. We've got a customer with a complaint. I came out to check his phone."

"Oh, you're with the complaint department? I was wondering why you weren't in a telephone truck."

He did some fast thinking. "Yeah, those repair guys get all the trucks. We have to use our own vehicles. We get paid for miles, though."

Thunder rumbled. Robin looked up. Less is more, he thought. Cool it with the small talk and get on with the job before she heads for the house to beat the rain.

"Well, looks like we might get that rain after all, huh? I guess I better try to find these folks. So, uh, do you know where Piney Woods Drive is?"

She scrunched her face. "Never heard of it."

"It's supposed to be around here somewhere. I've got a map, but I left my glasses at the office and the print on these maps is too small. It's all a blur. That's what happens when you get old. My kids make fun of my poor eyesight all the time. Do you think you could give it a quick look before the rain starts? I'd really appreciate it. Map's lying right here on the seat."

"Sure." She worked her way between the man and the car door. "You're lucky because I just got my new glasses yesterday or I couldn't read it either."

"How lucky can I get?" he said, smiling behind her as he pulled out the bottle, removed the cork, and tipped the liquid onto the rag.

As she leaned across the seat to reach for the map, she saw a pair of glasses on the floor and picked them up.

"Mister, I found your—" She froze when she saw the cracked, glued frame. It was her old pair of glasses.

He saw her pick up the glasses and knew he had to move

fast. With his elbow, he shoved her down against the seat and pinned her while he pressed the rag to her face. She struggled and kicked and tried to scream, but the rag muffled it. She was no match for a man double her weight.

As Robin slipped into unconsciousness, Alex and Marc reached her backyard. They panted and gasped for air as they looked around frantically. Parked along the road, two yards over, was the black SUV. Inside the open driver's door, a man struggled with something leaning on the driver's seat. When he moved slightly, they saw Robin's feet dangle beneath the open door.

"He's got Robin!" Marc said, pointing that way.

They dropped their bags and sprinted for the car.

Cooper heard them coming and turned to see the boys running his way full speed. He shoved Robin's limp body across the seat with an "umpf" and squeezed in behind the steering wheel. Before he could close the door, Marc grabbed it and wedged his body between it and the car. Alex saw Robin and ran to the other side to get her. Cooper turned the key in the ignition and the engine roared. He could easily speed off and leave the kids in the dust, but now they could identify him, too. He would have to take them with him.

While he fended off Marc's punches with his left arm, he reached under the seat for the pistol. As soon as his fingers closed on it, he whipped it out, and pressed it to Marc's face.

Marc felt the metal barrel press into his cheek and froze.

"Now listen and listen good. I want you and your friend over there to climb into the back seat *now* or I'll blow both your faces all over the pavement and never look back!"

Marc wasn't sure if Alex heard him, but was relieved when Alex opened the back door and climbed in. Marc reluctantly did the same.

Frank slammed his door and floored the accelerator. He hated it when things didn't go as planned. Meddlesome kids. He adjusted the rear view mirror so he could keep an eye on the two in the back and saw Alex staring at him.

He leaned toward the mirror. "Getting an eyeful, kid?"

The question startled Alex. His eyes jumped from the scar on the man's face to the angry eyes reflected in the mirror. He bit his lip and looked away.

Cooper grinned. *Oh, you won't have much longer to worry, kid. I'll see to that.*

The *Real* Bad Boy
✷ ✷ ✷ ✷ ✷ ✷

Bob Beekler listened to Detective Steve Owens' gravelly voice on his cell phone.

"Your wife is a detective's dream. She sketched the men to a T. They are Buster McClain and Frank Cooper. Buster works for the tire manufacturing plant in Madison. And get this, he drives a tanker truck and disposes toxic wastes."

Bob whistled as he stopped at the traffic light and stuffed the cell phone ear bud into his ear. "I'd say he's our man."

"We've got men posted at the tire plant gate," Owens said. "He'll be nabbed the minute he shows up. The most we've turned up on him is a few speeding violations. The real bad boy is Cooper. He has a rap sheet that fills a disk and he's probably the one who did the killing."

Bob noticed a black SUV coming in the opposite direction. The driver wore a dark ball cap. He turned across the intersection in front of him and headed up Highway 215 toward Salyersville. In the back seat were two boys. They were probably headed to a ball game, he thought. The light changed green and he accelerated towards Bridgeport.

"What's he done, Steve?"

"He's a hot one. Ol' Scar Face himself. Started with petty theft, graduated to grand larceny, did some time, was accused of murder but got off on a technicality. Says here he's obsessive-compulsive. A real neatness freak. Everything has to be just so or he comes unglued. I guess it takes a tidy mind to plan and commit crimes."

"What's he driving?"

"Don't know yet. Apparently just got a new vehicle, so it's taking a little longer. His old ride was a '97 dark blue Buick Century. That's what your niece saw by the cornfield that night."

"I'm on my way to Robin's now. I'll feel a whole lot better after I pick her up. Call me the second you get the make on the new car."

He pulled the receiver from his ear. His stomach was in knots. He knew Cooper would try to do away with Robin soon. He turned on the blue light and floored the accelerator. He had to get to Bridgeport and to Robin before Cooper did.

Fifteen minutes later he turned onto Maple Road and tensed when he saw a black pickup truck in front of Robin's house. He pulled up behind the truck and saw a big, silver-haired man bending down in the front yard.

He jumped out of the car and hurried towards him. As

the man straightened up, he recognized the Indian features.

"Kota," he said, "what are you doing here?"

"Looking for the kids."

Bob looked at the book bag in Kota's hand and the one at his feet. "Robin's not here?"

"I just drove up and found the bags. Robin's is over there by the road. I haven't gotten to the house yet. The police were supposed to be here, but I didn't see a squad car."

"Somebody was in a big hurry," Bob said, "if they left those bags out front like that."

They rushed to the front door. Kota rang the doorbell and asked, "Do you have a key? If not, I'll break it down."

Bob fumbled with his key ring, found the right one and opened the door. He ran from room to room calling Robin's name while Kota started at the opposite end of the house. When they met again in the living room, he looked at Kota who simply shook his head. He sank onto the couch and dropped his head in his hands.

Kota squeezed his shoulder. "We'll find them." He drew in a breath. "When Alex and Marc didn't get off the bus at their stop, the bus driver told me what happened. My guess is they saw something happen here on the street, got off, and tried to run back to Robin."

Bob rubbed his face. "It had to be Frank Cooper." He told him what Julie knew and what Detective Owens had told him. Then a woman's voice called from the doorway.

"Yoo-hoo."

When they turned, they saw a short, plump woman with pink sponge rollers in her graying hair.

"Excuse me. I'm Maggie Thurman from across the street." She pointed behind her with a hairbrush. "Blue house just over there. I've seen your cars here before, so I figure you know the family. Robin's such a sweet kid, you know. I wish I had half the hair she has."

This was the last thing Bob needed, but he politely asked, "Have you seen her?"

"Sorry about the way I look." She blushed, patting her rollers. "I was getting ready, but when I saw you drive up, I just wanted to make sure Robin was—all right."

"What do you mean 'all right'?" Kota said.

"Well, I was looking for the postman earlier and when I peeked out the window I saw her talking with a man by a car. One of them sports thingies that everybody's driving now. Those yuppie trucks. Seemed strange."

Kota stepped closer. "What was strange?"

"Robin was talking to him one minute and then the next she was flat gone. But he was standing there when the two boys ran up. I've seen them with Robin before."

"What about the boys?" Kota asked.

"One stayed on the driver's side. That was the tall black one. The other boy ran around to the passenger side and opened the front door. Looked like he was trying to move something in the seat. I don't know, though. But then he stopped, closed the door, and both boys got into the back seat. That's what I meant by strange. Kids like to ride in the front. My kids fight like cats and dogs over it. But the man was the only one I saw in the front and the two boys got in the back. And that was it. They drove away. A little too fast too, I might add. Why, the car screeched all the way down the street. It's a wonder he didn't turn that thing over and kill all of them. Some people are so reckless—and with kids in the car, too. I declare, you'd think they'd use better judgment. Where's the police when you need 'em?"

"So what happened to Robin?" Bob said.

She shrugged her shoulders. "I don't know. I couldn't figure out any of it. But the phone rang and when I looked again the car had disappeared. That's when I saw the book bags lying on the lawn, so I tried to call this house but nobody answered. That's when you drove up." She pointed to Kota. "And then you."

Bob's cell phone rang. He flipped it open. "Beekler."

"Owens again. We got the I.D. on Cooper's new car. It's a black SUV with an Indiana farm tag. Jefferson County, number SGHS-497." Bob scribbled the number on the back of his hand.

"Apparently he had one vehicle registered with his home address and the other registered at his place in the woods. Probably because farm licenses are cheaper."

"A black SUV," Bob said. "And we've got—"

Mrs. Thurman grabbed his arm and said, "That's it. He was wearing a baseball cap. Driving a black SUV."

His heart sank. "A ball cap?"

She nodded.

"Oh, Steve, I can't believe it! I saw them out on Highway 32."

Kota stared at him.

"I saw them turn in front of me when I was waiting at the light—while I was talking to you in fact. They turned onto Highway 215 heading north towards Salyersville."

"Gotta be taking them to the farm," Owens said. "Right outside Salyersville on Route 16. I'll get some cars up there right away and some dogs, too, since it's backed up to the state forest." Owens gave him some directions and hung up.

Bob closed the flip phone. "He's taking the kids to his place in Salyersville. It's next to the state forest. You coming?"

Kota was already heading for the door. "Wild Injuns couldn't keep me away."

A Nose for Money
❋ ❋ ❋ ❋ ❋ ❋

Stanley Edwards, Robin's stepfather, held his cell phone to his ear and peered nervously through the mini blinds of the Osage Tire Company. As plant supervisor he was responsible for all areas of operation, including the disposal of waste materials. He had thought he'd found a solution to his problems with the feds, one that would also stuff his pockets—illegal dumping of the toxic waste. That solution, however, was rapidly becoming worse than his marriage—possibly the worst nightmare of his life. The dumping operation had worked at first—until his wife's bratty kid stuck her nose in by finding the body. Then it hit the papers. When he had asked Buster and Cooper about it, they'd said they didn't know anything—their business was dumping. But now it was all getting too close to home.

He listened to the phone ring again and again while he waited for Buster to answer. Across the plant yard, he could see the plain-clothes detectives at the gate checking the tanker trucks as they came through. They had already questioned him about when Buster would show up for work. Stan knew the cops were onto something and knew if Buster got caught he would implicate him.

After six rings Buster answered. Stanley didn't give him a chance to speak before whispering into the mouthpiece. "Buster, it's me, down at the factory. Just listen, I don't have much time. Don't come near this place. It's crawling with cops looking for you. If you show up, they'll nab you. Your trailer's probably covered too, so don't go there. Where are you?"

"I was on my way in to pick up the truck. I'm on I-65, near the last rest stop before town. You know, the one where we first set everything up."

"Yeah, I remember. But forget the last truck. I'll just do it through the company. It's the cash I'm worried about. I want that out of my hands in case they start searching the office. And Buster, I do not want my butt dragged into this! Do you understand?"

"Gotcha. I'll wait for ya at the rest stop."

At the rest stop, Stan Edwards got out of his car and jumped into Buster's rusty station wagon with a blue gym bag. Buster eyed the bag stuffed with bills. A sense of excitement bubbled inside him. Not once had he pictured himself as the one to receive the cash. Cooper was going to handle that.

Stan handed over the bag and Buster started to open it. "Don't count it here," Stan said, watching a young couple walk past on their way to the restrooms. "It's all there, trust me. Mostly hundreds and about a third in twenties, minus twenty grand for me."

"That's the first I've heard about twenty grand," Buster said, staring at him. "You already got your cut."

"I did, but that was before you guys screwed things up by getting the cops involved. Now my butt's on the line. And I don't even want to know how Dyer got killed."

Buster certainly wasn't going to say anything about it. While Stan talked and people came and went, starting engines and slamming doors, he thought about the money. One hundred-eighty thousand divided by two was still a lot of cash.

"If I had that much," Stan said, "I'd leave my miserable wife and her pesky kid." He rubbed his day's growth of beard. "Might do it anyway. By the way, what are you going to do with all that money?"

Buster unzipped the bag a little, stuck his nose to the opening, and sniffed. They smelled like fast cars, lots of chicks, and a regular spot at the casino. When he came up for air, he said, "First thing, I guess, is to give Cooper his half."

"Cooper? Don't you listen to the news, Buster? The cops are on him like stink on a wet dog! They think they have him trapped up in the woods near Salyersville. You might as well write him off, Buster. He's history."

Buster went numb as he stared at Stan. He looked out the windshield as the rain began to patter and slide down the glass. *What was Cooper doing?* That wasn't the plan. He was supposed to release the kid at the rest stop. At least that's what he'd told him. And what if he got caught? He'd go to prison and take me down with him. He clutched the canvas bag and heard Stan's voice.

"You mind what I say, Buster. Take that money and get outta town—fast! Get to Mexico or anywhere, but don't go home. I don't want the police to end up knocking on my door. Leave now and never come back."

His mind reeled. He thought of his dilapidated trailer. He looked down at the sack of cash. "Okay, okay. I'll hit the road, now!"

Stan slid out of the car into the rain.

Buster started the engine and thought about his job at the factory, about the people in the town who always made fun of him, and he thought about Cooper who always bossed him around, and treated him like the scum of the earth. But he wasn't as stupid as Cooper thought he was.

He turned on the wipers and watched the rubber strips slap at the raindrops. He had always been like those little drops—always pushed to the side. But not anymore. From now on things would be different. He patted the bag, lowered it to the floorboard, and backed out of the parking spot.

When he merged into the traffic heading south on Interstate 65 he was finally able to relax. He breathed the refreshing smell of rain that filtered in through the vent. On the radio he heard the D.J. announce, "You're listening to the Golden Oldies on Y108." He changed the station. He was leaving the past behind. For the first time in his life, he was free, in charge, and rich! $180,000 rich!

On the Run

✳ ✳ ✳ ✳ ✳ ✳

Bob's dusty brown Explorer sped along Highway 32 with the blue emergency light flashing in the fading daylight. He slowed at the intersection of Highway 215, made a left turn, and picked up speed. As he drove, he brought Kota up to date.

"I've been on Route 16," Kota said. "There are a few cabins and some small houses—all pretty spread out."

Thick raindrops splattered the windshield.

"Oh, that's great," Bob turned on the wipers. The blades swiped back and forth across the glass, slapping water from side to side.

"Steve said Cooper's cabin is just past the Y in the road. Supposed to be about a hundred yards down on the left. They have no idea if the other guy's going to be there, but he's small potatoes. Cooper's the real bad one. He's the one with the beard and the scar running down his face. He could have shaved the beard, but there's no hiding that scar."

He felt for the revolver he'd loaded back at Robin's house and found it secure in the holster. "You'll find another gun under the seat, Kota."

"Won't need it," Kota said, whipping out the twelve-inch blade. Bob jerked the steering wheel and the car swerved momentarily onto the shoulder.

"May look big," Kota remarked, "but it can split hairs."

"Whoa, fella," Bob said, wiping his forehead. "Take it easy with that thing. Wouldn't a gun be better?"

"Nope."

Bob opened the window a little and continued, "They're bringing dogs. If he runs for the woods we'll be able to track him."

"Dogs? Dogs are noisy and they announce where the tracker is."

Bob became quiet. He had never encountered anyone quite like Kota. In the silence, the windshield wipers metronomed the miles as they sped along the wet highway to Salyersville.

Robin was still unconscious when Cooper pulled off Route 16 and maneuvered the winding driveway to the cabin. He stopped the car and waved the gun towards the back seat. "Looks like you guys are stuck with carrying your sleepy friend."

They stared at him. Getting out of the SUV might not be

a good idea. They shouldn't have gotten in to begin with.

"I guess you didn't hear me," Cooper said, jerking open Marc's door and shoving the gun against his ear. "Maybe I need to open up your ears a little."

Alex pulled the handle and scrambled out. The cold rain and fall air made him gasp. Marc scooted across the seat and out behind him. Rain ran down their faces and into their eyes and pattered the leaves on the ground. Alex opened the front passenger door and caught Robin as she fell sideways.

"She's dead!" Alex gasped.

"No she's not, you fool," Cooper snapped. "Not yet anyway."

Alex and Marc exchanged concerned looks as they eased Robin out of the car. She was heavy and as limp as a rag doll. They hooked her arms around their necks and hauled her around the SUV, dragging her feet along the ground.

Cooper signaled them to the house. He led them inside to the tiled entryway and motioned with the gun for them to take off their shoes.

Marc couldn't believe the guy was concerned about a little dirt at a time like this. They each managed to stand on one foot and remove their shoes while balancing Robin between them.

Cooper straightened and aligned each pair of sneakers. "And don't forget hers!"

Marc supported her weight while Alex slipped off her shoes. Then they carried her to the couch, covered with plastic, and eased her down.

Marc and Alex looked around anxiously. The place was spotless. White walls, white cabinets, white furniture and even white carpet. Not a typical cabin in the woods.

The boys sat on the couch with Robin between them. Her head lay on the back of the couch with her mouth wide open.

The rain tapped at the window, making Alex wish he were out in it. He looked around for another exit and saw a back door in the kitchen. He also saw a cordless phone on the kitchen counter and felt a glimmer of hope. His mind ran through the possibilities of what might happen. The guy could just tie them up and leave town. It depended on whether he was planning to stay or run. Either way, they could identify him. It soon became very clear to Alex that the man would have to kill and bury them deep in the woods. No, burying three would be too much trouble. He'd just march them deep in the woods and shoot them. Their bodies would never be found. And he'd never be identified. He would not only get away with Seth's murder, but theirs as well.

Alex felt sick to his stomach. He watched the guy pop the tab on a diet cola and take a big gulp, not offering them anything. When he stopped drinking, his eyes locked on Alex. His face, especially his eyes, were pure evil. The eyes of a killer—his killer.

"Always staring, aren't ya kid? Couldn't leave well enough alone, could you? All of you."

The tone and crazy look in his eyes sent shivers down Alex's back. The man started walking towards them. Alex held his breath. *What was he going to do?* He stopped at the coffee table and pressed the power button on the remote. Alex exhaled as the TV blinked from black to living color.

"If I were you boys I'd wake up your sleepy friend, unless you want to be carrying her again."

So they were leaving, Alex thought. *The car? Or the woods?*

While he and Marc tried to wake Robin, the local news anchorman appeared on the TV with a breaking story.

"Police are currently searching for this man off Route 16 near the Kirk National Forest." A picture of Cooper filled the screen. "His name is Frank Cooper and he is wanted in connection with the kidnapping of three middle-school students." Cooper quickly turned up the volume.

Alex and Marc stared at the screen.

The police knew about them! Alex chanced a look at Marc who gawked at the TV. *And the guy's name was Frank Cooper.*

The anchorman continued, "He is considered armed and dangerous."

No kidding! Alex thought. *The sketch was an exact duplicate, down to the earring.*

Frank Cooper stood slack-jawed. A vein on the side of his neck bulged.

"He is also wanted in connection with the recent murder of local farmer Seth Dyer."

Cooper's hands balled into fists.

A different sketch appeared on the screen.

"A second man, Buster McClain, is also wanted and considered armed and dangerous. Both are also suspected of illegally dumping a toxic substance known as PERC."

The newscaster adjusted his earpiece. "We now have names and photos of the kidnapped students." Their school pictures flashed onto the screen. Alex grimaced. If he got out of this alive, he was going to destroy every school picture of him in town.

"They are Robin Beekler, Marc Corby, and Alex Sanders, all students at Bridgeport Middle School."

Cooper turned off the TV, then threw the remote across the room. It smashed against the wall and the small black pieces scattered onto the tile floor. He stomped into an adjoining room, slamming the door behind him.

Alex sat bolt upright, his heart pounding. Cooper had left the gun on the counter! This was their chance. Alex signaled Marc to lift Robin and he darted for the gun. He was nearly there when Cooper suddenly appeared through another door and cut him off. Cooper slapped him across the face, knocking him sideways. "That wasn't so smart, was it kid?"

Alex's face stung. He pressed it with his hand. When he looked back at Cooper, he was so close he could see his nose hairs.

"You can believe I won't make that mistake again."

Alex backed to the couch and slumped onto the seat.

Marc lowered Robin onto the couch. She was like dead weight. He had to wake her up or they could never make a break for it. Marc patted her face and shook her shoulders. They were running out of time now that Cooper knew the police were looking for him.

The man waved the gun around, telling them not to move. He grabbed a duffel bag from the hall closet and disappeared into the other room. Marc worked feverishly on Robin.

"Maybe some water would help," Alex whispered.

Cooper appeared in the doorway. "What are you talking about?"

"I was just saying," Alex said, "that maybe some water would help wake her up. And I need to go to the bathroom."

"Bathroom!" He raised the gun. "Get in there." He waved the gun towards a door off the kitchen. "And put down the lid when you're done!"

What a freak! Alex thought as he headed for the bathroom. As he closed the door, he looked around frantically for a weapon.

Cooper yelled through the door and startled him. "And

be sure to wash your hands! I can't stand germs!"

Alex made a face over his shoulder. He flushed the toilet and turned on the faucet so Cooper would hear it running. Then he started going through the drawers. Nothing in the small drawer to the left. He opened the one on the right. Bingo! Lying in little plastic compartments were a small pair of scissors and a metal nail file. He stuck them in his jeans pocket, closed the drawer, and turned off the water.

When he opened the door he nearly ran into Cooper who had apparently been listening at the door!

Alex swallowed hard.

"Show me your hands," Cooper demanded.

Alex blinked. *The guy was nuts.* And he hadn't washed his hands at all because he was too busy looking for a weapon. He held his breath and held up his hands. Cooper grabbed his wrists and turned them over. To Alex's relief he pronounced them clean. Weak-kneed, Alex returned to the couch.

Then Marc very politely said, "Mister—"

"Cooper."

"Mister Cooper, could I go to the bathroom, too—please?"

"My, aren't we polite now? Do it fast and remember what I said about the lid."

Marc hurried to the bathroom. When he flushed, he reached above the toilet and unlocked the window. Then, remembering the inspection Alex went through, he quickly washed his hands and when he opened the door he held them up. He was surprised to see them shaking.

"Good." Cooper growled. "Now sit down. And don't be such a scaredy-cat. Behave and you'll live."

Cooper went into the bathroom. Alex heard him open a drawer and close it. He held his breath. *Which one had he opened?* The man strode towards them with something in his hand.

Alex braced himself for another hit. To his surprise, Cooper shoved something at Marc.

"Use this. It's an ammonia capsule. It'll bring her around. Just break it open and shove it under her nose."

When Cooper walked off, Alex slumped in relief.

Marc stood and did as he was told, holding it under Robin's nose till she stirred and slapped his hand away.

"Wake up!" Marc urged under his breath.

Robin's eyes blinked open.

Alex pulled her glasses from his pocket and slid them onto her face. "I saw them in the car when we were getting out so I grabbed 'em."

Robin adjusted her glasses. "Where are we?"

Before the boys could answer, Cooper returned and dropped two bulging bags by the door. He looked at Robin.

"*Where are we?*" he mimicked. "Why, you're in Kansas, Dorothy," he said, waving his arms. "Or soon will be. So get on your feet. We're taking a little field trip."

Oh no, Alex thought. *Kirk National Forest.*

Marc and Alex helped Robin to her feet when Cooper said, "Quiet! What was that?" He held up a hand. "Listen." Something thumped outside. *A car door?* Dogs barked. Doors slammed.

Marc looked at Alex. *The police! They made it.*

Cooper ran to the front window, flattened himself against the wall, and lifted the edge of the curtain. He quickly turned back to them, pulled a roll of duct tape from his jacket pocket, and taped their mouths shut and their hands together. He threw their shoes at them. "Put 'em on," he ordered.

They struggled to help each other.

"Alright kids, we've got some traveling to do." He herded them to the back of the house and peered through the panes in the door. "I'll only tell you this once. When I open this, you head straight for the woods, and if I see you try anything else I'm going to shoot you and just keep running. Have I made myself clear?"

They nodded.

Cooper twisted the doorknob, looked again, and jerked it open. In a low voice, he said, "Go!" He shoved the kids into the pouring rain.

One after the other, they rushed across the open yard to the thicket of woods behind the cabin. It wasn't far, but with their mouths taped shut they were wheezing and snorting like spent horses by the time they were twenty feet inside the tree line.

Marc led the group into the woods and with each step, he hoped someone would yell out, *"Police! Stop!"* But no one did. Instead he heard his own footsteps and heavy breathing along with the steady drumming of the rain. He also heard frogs croaking and crickets chirping while they slipped deeper and deeper into the darkened woods.

Marc's clothes sopped water like a sponge and quickly became so heavy he felt as though he had rocks in his pockets. His taped hands threw him off balance, and he wobbled from side to side as he slogged through the mud. He tried to open his mouth to loosen the tape, but it was stuck fast. His breath came harder and his lungs filled with the scent of rain, wet earth, and leaves. He tried to fix the scent in his mind. After all, it could be the last thing he ever smelled.

Alex wondered about his grandfather. Surely the police had told him. He remembered his grandfather telling him to call on the spirit world whenever he needed help. Well, this was certainly the time. He tried to concentrate, but that was hard with the slippery, muddy ground, and with the metal barrel of the gun continually thrust against his back.

"Spirits do listen," his grandfather had told him. "Just send thoughts out into the universe." Alex tried to visualize them floating up and being caught in a spirit dream catcher. *Bring Grandpa! Please—before it's too late!*

Time passed. They trudged further and further into the woods and to his dismay, nothing extraordinary happened. No genie or angel appeared. No Grandpa. As the minutes passed, his spirit sank. Each step was harder, his shoes heavier. He was so hungry he felt nauseated. If he spit up with the tape on his mouth, he could choke to death. He began to wonder if the spirit world listened to thirteen-year-old boys.

Rain soaked Robin's hair and trickled down her face onto her sodden flannel shirt and jeans. Her sneakers were so mud-coated they were like skates. She stumbled over exposed roots and got snagged by briars. *Where were the roads and mulched paths they took on field trips?*

She tried to peer through the ever-darkening woods to find something familiar. But this was real wilderness— beyond anything she'd ever known. This was beyond the roads Kota talked about—the Red and the Black Roads. She was in the Black Nowhere.

She followed closely behind Marc and prayed for many things. Prayed for rescue. For dry clothes. For food. For daylight. *Where were the police? Were they going to die? In the middle of nowhere, never to be found?* She never thought her life would end so soon or like this. She was supposed to be a doctor and the first woman president, like Mr. Michaels always said.

There had to be a way out. She couldn't just give up. She had to do something. But what? She couldn't run fast or jump high or throw anything hard or accurately like Marc and Alex. All she had was brains and a will to live, although that was diminishing with each step. If their rescue was up to her, they were in big trouble.

She remembered what Kota told her about the Lakota people and how their culture had survived. It was by walking Grandmother's Road, a road of quiet fortitude—a grandmother's weapon—an inner strength that drew upon bravery and wisdom. That's what saved a person in the face of adversity. She had to think strong and think brave.

Something wriggly landed on her cheek and crawled onto her neck. *Spider!* She screamed but the tape garbled the sound. She tried to brush the creature away. It dropped—on the ground, she hoped. Her heart pounded in her chest. It was all too much. The rain, bugs, a killer, and whatever lay ahead. She couldn't let herself think about it. She had to remember Grandmother's Road, and quiet strength, so she could think of some way out.

She looked around for options, but it was so dark. Her mother always told her not to fear the dark. Well, right now, with the creepy sounds and insects, the cold rain and a gun pointed at her, she wasn't so sure. Besides, what if she did get away from Cooper? Could she find her way out? She remembered what Kota said about how the Lakota always watched their back trail so they could recognize the way home. She looked around. Too dark to see a thing.

"Hurry!" Cooper said for what seemed like the millionth time. "Get up that incline."

Robin heard Marc thrash and groan. He was entangled in a briar bush. She tried to help him, but was pricked by the thorns.

Cooper grabbed him by the belt and jerked him out of the briars. A sound escaped from beneath the duct tape and Cooper shoved Marc back onto the trail.

Alex knew Marc was getting the worst of it, but he wasn't about to trade places. He continued his mantra to the spirits and thought of the dogs. Why hadn't he heard the dogs? Then he realized their scents and footprints had been washed away, soaked into the forest floor, and absorbed by every tree and plant as if they'd never been there.

There was a sudden splashy thump ahead. Marc had hit the ground. Poor Marc. The name reverberated in his brain. Marc. Mark. Mark. *Mark the trail!* His grandfather had reminded him of that just days ago when they found Seth. Why hadn't he thought of it sooner? But how far had they gone without marking anything? Would Grandpa find the first one this far out? A calmness settled around him like a cloud. The spirit world would bring his Grandpa.

Alex could make out the form of a small tree a few feet ahead. As he passed, he reached to the side and broke a branch, bending it in the direction they were heading and walked on. Cooper said nothing. He must not have noticed.

Alex sent thanks into the air and sent thoughts like arrows to his grandfather. *U wo, Tunkaśila. You've got to come.* He hoped those arrows hit their mark.

Minutes later, Alex stumbled into Robin who had collided with Marc. In the path was a stand of large oaks that had grown together. Cooper told them to take a right. As Alex did so, he broke another branch, marking the direction.

Twenty feet later, Cooper warned them about a drop up ahead. When they reached it, they slid down on their behinds. In a short while, they crossed a shallow creek. Alex had the feeling Cooper wasn't just running away. He had a destination.

When Alex got into the water, he pretended to slip. When he went down, he raked the creek bottom for pebbles and put them in his pocket. When he reached the other side, he pretended to slip again and placed three stones to point the way.

When Bob and Kota pulled into the yard at the cabin they found four police cars and two barking dogs straining for a possum trail. Bob could see the frustration in Kota's face.

"Bob, do you have a flashlight?" Kota asked.

Bob got him one from the back of the car and they joined Detective Owens and the County Sheriff, John Jacobs, who were leaning over a map on the hood of a car.

"We'll place a man here, here, here, and here," the sheriff said, pointing to the map. A deputy held a flashlight and umbrella over it.

"The thing to remember," the sheriff said, "is this property is backed up to a thousand acres of virgin forest. If he passes the perimeter it's going to be next to impossible to catch him."

"John," Owens said, "you're crazy if you don't cover this area here."

Kota knew a man like Cooper wouldn't sit around and wait for them to come get him. He would make his own move, which might involve killing the kids. Kota had to act. So while the police continued to plan as though they were invading Iraq, he backed away and slipped into the woods unnoticed.

He crept among the trees and studied the sides and back of the house. Only one light in the front. Fortunately, his night vision was like a cat's. In the backyard, he found a toolshed. Leaning against it was Robin's bike.

He crouched low and ran back across the grass to the house where he tested each window. When he found the bathroom window unlocked, he raised it slowly, adjusted his knife, and hoisted himself up and squeezed inside, careful not to make noise.

He stepped down off the toilet seat and stood behind the bathroom door where he listened. Something ticked. He swallowed hard. The thought of a bomb tied to one of the kids crossed his mind. But it was simply a thought, not an image. Very different things for someone with extra sight.

He listened and waited. Nothing. With three kids and a nervous killer in the house, he should have heard something—a footstep, a cough, anything. Through the crack in the door, he could see only a sliver of the couch in the living room. Finally he placed a hand on the door and pulled. As the space widened, his eyes swept the room. There was no one there.

Kota watched the floor for shadows, took a breath, and stepped into the room. Again, nothing. He checked the rest of the cabin. Cooper had gotten away and taken the kids with him.

He headed for the front door to tell the others and saw the two duffel bags. Through the window he saw the officers still leaning over the map. There was no time. No time to convince them to move. He would have to track them alone. It was the best chance for the kids.

He felt the couch. Not warm, but on the back he found red hairs and on the seat found the smelling salts. Robin had been unconscious. That was why the neighbor hadn't seen her sitting in the car.

He saw the duct tape on the glass-top coffee table. Cooper probably taped their hands and mouths so they wouldn't yell out. Couldn't tape their feet though or they wouldn't be able to walk. He grabbed a pad and pen from the counter and scribbled a note for Bob. When he was finished, he slipped out the back and into the woods.

Inside the tree line, Kota searched for signs. He finally found footprints protected by an overhang of bushes. He was on the right path. He moved in a crouching stance for some time, dodging bushes and stumps, and stopped suddenly when the image of a broken branch appeared in his mind. He smiled and studied the bushes to his right where he discovered a broken branch. Ah *Mitakoja*, you remembered! He thanked *Wakan Tanka*.

Knowing Alex would mark the path when they changed direction, he picked up his pace. He felt the spirit of the wolf course through his body and was soon deep into the forest.

When the police finally stormed the cabin, it was empty. Bob buried his face in his hands till one of the deputies called his name.

"Look at this," he said, handing Bob the note.

Bob read it and breathed a sigh of relief tinged with regret. He wished Kota had taken him, but it would have been difficult for both of them to leave without being noticed. Besides, he was bound by protocol.

Good for you, Kota! he thought. *And Godspeed.* In the background Bob heard the sheriff.

"Who does he think he is—The Lone Ranger? This is police business."

Bob grinned as he passed the note to Steve Owens.

"Well," the sheriff said, "I hope the dang fool doesn't get hisself or the kids killed. Get the dogs. We better head out after 'em."

"It's still pouring," said one of the dog handlers. "Dogs can't pick up anything now. Have to wait till it lets up."

The sheriff slammed his hat down on the counter. "Then we'll just wait. The minute it lets up we're heading out." He began to pace. "There's no telling what's going to happen out there now."

Bob had reached his limit. "Sheriff, Kota knows what he's doing. He's a Lakota Indian who's been tracking all his life, and he would never risk the lives of those kids. One is his grandson. One is my niece. Thank God he was brave enough to go out there in the dark to find them." He looked at the others. "Truth is, he might have a better shot at it alone. I pity anyone he's after."

The sheriff put his hat back on. "Let's hope you're right, Bob. For all their sakes."

The Long Night
✽ ✽ ✽ ✽ ✽ ✽

Midnight came and went and Cooper and the kids still trudged through the woods. Cooper found their progress irritatingly slow, but didn't know whether the kids were intentionally dragging their feet or plain worn out. They hadn't eaten, so they were probably weak. He watched Robin struggle up an incline. She tried to grab some branches with her taped hands, but lost her grip. Within minutes, she slid down the embankment and right into him.

He jerked her to her feet. "Get your worthless butt back up that hill!" He ought to just shoot 'em all and be done with it, but he had a better plan.

Robin grumbled through the tape. Cooper stared down at her. They could probably move faster if they could breathe better. In one quick motion, he ripped the tape off her mouth.

She gasped while pressing her fingers to her lips. "Ouch!"

Alex couldn't believe his ears. Her tape was off. And her voice sounded angry. He hoped she wouldn't say anything stupid.

"What is it?" Cooper growled.

"You keep yelling at us to hurry, but our hands are bound together and we can hardly breathe, and the mud's so thick it's hard to stand up, let alone walk. You ever try to climb a hill with your wrists taped?"

"Well, that's just too bad, isn't it, Little Red?"

She was not only exhausted, she was fed up. "You think you're so tough, don't you, just because you can pick on poor defenseless ki—"

Cooper backhanded her, sending her flat onto the mud. Stunned, she sat up, shaking her head.

Alex knelt down to see if she was okay. Meanwhile Marc charged for Cooper, but stopped when the man pulled the pistol from his waistband.

"That's two strikes. One more and you're out. Now step back and help Big Mouth to her feet."

Alex struggled to help.

Robin's knees went weak as she thought about how Marc could have been shot. And it would have been her fault, like everything else.

Robin was cold and achy, and covered in mud as thick as pancake batter. Her cheek burned where Cooper had slugged her. Most of all, she was scared she was going to die. All of them were. Cooper's voice interrupted her thoughts.

"You know, Red, you might have a point. I'll take off the tape and see how much faster you kids move. If you can't pick up the pace, well, then I'll just have to take other measures because I'm getting out of here one way or another."

He ripped the tape from Alex's mouth and did the same to Marc. He pulled a pocketknife from his jacket and slit the tape on their wrists. He had the urge to whack Robin again. Instead, he rammed the pistol under her chin, pushing her head back at a painful angle. "Any more of that smart mouth and I'll blow it off. Now get yourself in gear and haul butt." He shoved her into the lead and told the others to follow.

While they trudged along, Cooper tried to figure things out. The police must have stormed the cabin by now and entered the woods, but he hadn't heard any dogs. That meant there was a delay, probably because of the rain and darkness. And even if they brought out the dogs, the rain would have washed away their scents.

The police would figure he wouldn't get very far with the kids in tow. Cooper watched them pick up the pace and was glad he removed the tape. He was also glad he decided to double back across the creek and walk upstream another hundred feet. With a thousand acres of forest, a drenching rain, and the head start, he definitely had a leg up on the police and the dogs, if they ever got to use the dogs.

When the kids tried to get up a steep slope, they kept sliding back on the leaves and mud. They climbed some and slid, climbed more, and slid again. Robin and Marc finally made it to a level area and collapsed. Alex was about to crest it when he lost his footing and slid back down the bumpy slope. His fingers raked the ground as he tried to find something to grab. He slid further and further down until he passed Cooper and thumped against a tree trunk.

Cooper yelled, "Get up."

Alex was wracked with pain. At first, he couldn't move. Finally he got up and tried the slope again. This time he climbed parallel to the slippery path, using clumps of weeds as footholds and low branches as grips that he bent to mark the trail.

When they all reached the plateau, Cooper said, as if they would be glad to hear it, "We're almost there. It's just over that knoll."

Dead Horse Point was the perfect place to do away with the kids. The thousand-foot drop would be the end of them. No bullets. No evidence. A clean kill. From this direction and in the dark they would not have a clue about the sheer drop. It was a rock slab at the top of a rock wall. In daylight it was a spectacular view of the forest, the lake in the distance, and the rocky ground a thousand feet below. Too bad the kids wouldn't see the view on their way down.

All he had to do was tell them to go straight. The one leading again, little "Mohammed Ali" would go first. If the other two balked, he'd force them to the edge with his gun—or just push. Couldn't be easier, except for that squirrely red-headed brat. He thought of the police. If they were making any headway, a hostage or two would come in handy.

His heart quickened as the kids approached the top. He had to make a decision. He considered his options. If they found him with the kids, the charge would be kidnapping. If they went over the edge, the charge would be murder. What was the difference? He'd already killed the farmer. How many life sentences could he serve? Life was life. Besides, everybody dies at some point. Hostages would only slow him down. Just herd 'em over the edge and be done. He could see Marc stepping onto the rock ledge.

Kota hurried along as the rain slackened. He had time to make up. Time he had lost at the creek when Cooper had doubled back. That was a savvy move. He'd been pursued before. Fortunately, Kota found the stones pointing the way. He couldn't wait to get his hands on Cooper, or get within twenty feet for a clear shot with his knife.

As Marc stepped into a clearing, he felt a rocky surface beneath his feet and a strong breeze ruffle his shirt. He stopped abruptly, causing Robin and Alex to bump into him, knocking him forward. As he fell, his elbows and body slammed onto a rocky ledge. A strong updraft of air pressed against his face and hands and he realized he was hanging partway over it. He gasped and scrambled backwards into the others. "Stop! There's a cliff edge!" he yelled.

Alex panicked and grabbed the back of Marc's shirt, pulling with all his might. "Back, Robin!" he said. "Move back!" *Cooper wanted them to fall over the edge!* Alex had to find another direction fast, but which way? Right? Left?

A gust of wind blew from the left. It was the Sign. *Follow the wind,* it said—blowing his hair to the right. It would take a leap of faith.

Cooper panicked when he realized they were already on the ledge. He had decided he needed bargaining chips in case the police caught up with him. A kid for a car. Another for a plane. The last one for anything unforeseen. At least till he was out of the country and in Costa Rica. Then he would contact Stan and collect the money. *The money! Buster! Did he finish the job? Did he get away? What about the money?*

"Stop! Wait," Cooper yelled. "There's a thousand-foot drop over the edge! Turn right."

Right? Alex thought. He wasn't about to trust a killer. If he said right, they must have to go left. After all, he tried to run them off the edge. *But the spirit sign said right.* He didn't know what to do. It would all be so easy for Cooper if they fell. No gunshots—nothing. That was why Cooper had brought them up there. Yet, Alex had to trust his inner spirit.

He grabbed Marc's hand and placed it onto the back of his belt. Then he slid his foot to the right, making sure the ground was solid. He steadied himself while Marc continued to hold him and slid his foot again, testing the ground like a blind man. Again he felt the rock surface beneath him. With his next slide he felt weeds and smelled earth. They were on a slope heading down.

When they reached level ground, the rain had tapered off. They were making their way through a stand of sycamores and pines when there was a deep bellowing sound.

Robin grabbed Alex.

"What was that?" she said.

"A frog. Now get off. You're choking me."

Gripping tighter, she said, "That was no frog."

"It was a frog," he insisted, trying to pull her arms from around his neck.

"It's a mountain lion," Robin squealed.

Cooper grabbed her by the hair. "It's a bullfrog, you idiot. Now get off him and walk."

She loosened her grip, but stuck close to Alex who coughed and rubbed his throat.

"You're a pain in the butt, brat," Cooper hissed.

She didn't reply, keeping her eyes on the bushes. Behind them, the gray and white trunks of sycamores lined the trail.

They continued to trudge through dense woods till they came to a slight clearing with weeds. After a short distance, they stumbled onto the steps of a small, dark cabin.

Cooper hurried ahead. His shoes thumped up the steps and clumped across a porch. Before they knew it, the door creaked open and he shoved them inside.

One by one, they cautiously crossed the threshold.

Robin was last. She hesitated on the porch after Marc and Alex had gone in. *What's a cabin doing in a state forest?* she wondered.

"Just get inside," Cooper barked, waving his gun and scanning the clearing to see if they'd been followed.

Every cell in her body told Robin not to cross that threshold. She looked at the pistol, then stepped into dank, musty darkness. Marc pulled her between them.

"We finally made it kiddos. Welcome to the stopover in our little field trip. Or maybe it's your final destination. Depends on your behavior."

They backed against the studs and listened to Cooper clomp back and forth across the wooden floor. Something rattled in a box, slid, and scraped. A small flame sparked above Cooper's fingers. It was the first light they had seen in hours. The match illuminated his face and hand. He looked tired and dirty, but the diamond earring still sparkled on his ear. He walked to a kerosene lamp on a wooden box and touched the match to the wick. It flamed to life, bathing the cabin in a dim, yellow haze. Then he lit another one next to a wooden seat. The room brightened.

He knelt at the hearth and made a fire. Marc, Alex, and Robin stole glances around the cabin while trying not to draw attention to themselves. The whole place was the size of a living room. The few tables, benches, and stools were hewn from split logs. Everything in the cabin was unfinished, natural wood and bathed in firelight.

Robin was stupefied. She figured they'd been heading for a car or boat Cooper had stowed away somewhere. She couldn't believe he was making a fire. *Smoke in a state forest? The rangers would be on them like flies to sugar.* She felt a glimmer of hope till she wondered why he wasn't still trying to get away. For some reason, she felt more chilled in the cabin than she had outside.

While crouched in front of the fire, Cooper pivoted to face them. He looked at Robin and smiled.

"Really got you stumped, hasn't it Little Red? You're the analytical one. Always trying to figure things out." He set the box of matches on the mantel. "For your information, we're not on federal property anymore. We're on the outskirts. The guy who used to own this little place kept the fire roaring all the time." He chuckled. "Obviously he doesn't now, does he?" He picked up the metal poker. "I own it. You might say I won it in a poker game." He laughed at his private joke as he poked the fire.

Bob Beekler called Robin's mother and explained what had happened. Then he called Karen Sanders. He told her about the police delay, but added that Kota was already in the woods tracking them.

"He's not as young as he used to be," Karen said. "And it's so dark. Anything could happen out there in the woods —with that killer."

"The dogs'll pick up their trail at daybreak," Bob said.

"Have they found the other man, that Buster guy?"

"Not a sign of him. I'll let you know if there's any news. I still need to call Marc's parents."

"They're sitting right here in the kitchen with me. I'll fill them in. Thanks for calling."

Just as he hung up he saw Detective Owens and the sheriff return from the woods.

"What's the word, Steve?" Bob asked, grabbing the detective's elbow. "Could you tell where they went?"

Owens kicked his boot against the tire to knock off the mud. "You can hardly stand up in that mess or even see the hand in front of your face with all those trees and the cloud cover." He shook his head. "We couldn't get fifty feet without falling over one another or getting tangled in the briars. We'll have to wait till daybreak." He rubbed his neck and turned the collar up on his jacket. "I'm afraid it's gonna be a long night."

It wasn't what Bob wanted to hear. "Did you see any

signs of Kota?"

"Not a feather," the sheriff smirked.

Bob didn't laugh.

"He just disappeared into the woods same as Cooper and the kids." The sheriff clucked his tongue. "That forest is like a black hole."

Kota lost the trail. In desperation, he switched on the flashlight and held it low to the ground. The beam of light spilled over a patchwork of footprints and stones pointing toward a steep incline. Relieved, Kota switched off the light and tucked it back into his belt. He angled his way to the side of the slippery path using the weeds as footholds to climb.

Halfway up the hill Kota stopped to catch his breath. Another bent branch urged him on. A break in the trees ahead indicated he was near the crest of a hill.

He felt a spurt of adrenaline and hurried the last few feet to the clearing. The hard rock surface now beneath him meant he could move faster. He started running when bats fluttered in his face, startling him. *Bats.* More rose from below in a ghostly cloud. They swished so close, in a flurry of wings and screeching sounds, that he had to duck to the ground. When he did, his boot slid over the edge. He froze. He had an urge to turn on the flashlight, but at the top of a hill, it would be like a beacon signaling Cooper that he was on the trail. He felt along the rock and found a dropoff, but how much? A few feet? A hundred? He felt an updraft and sniffed. The air smelled like primeval steam rising from rock and forest far below.

He set down the flashlight and shifted onto his haunches so he could feel around for a stone. He found one near his foot, picked it up and tossed it over the edge. There was a long eerie silence, then a distant tink, tink, tink, as the stone bounced far below.

His body went weak. *The kids! Had they fallen over?* Cooper might have brought them up here for that purpose—to be rid of them. The idea made him dizzy, till he realized he would have been close enough to hear them scream—unless they were still gagged.

The faces of the three kids flashed in his head. It was an image from his spirit guides telling him they were still alive. He needed to hurry, but which way? Left or right? Or had Cooper doubled back again? Had he come here for the sole purpose of eliminating those tracking him?

Kota felt around for more stones. He tossed one to the left and waited. In the seconds that followed he wondered if there was water below. He finally heard the barest sound—
—rock against rock—and far away. He was at the edge of a precipice. *Good God. It was Dead Horse Point.* He should have remembered.

A bird trilled notes off to his right. He cocked his head. A Blue Jay? In the dead of night? Another sign! As a precaution he tossed a stone and it immediately chinked along rocky ground. Without hesitating, he hurried across the rock onto a grassy path and headed down a slope.

Marc, Alex, and Robin huddled together on a bench in the sparsely furnished one-room cabin. Pots and cups hung between the studs on the wall. Boards nailed between the studs served as shelves for canned goods and a few dishes. Robin didn't see a bathroom and she felt like she was going to pop, but was afraid to ask. Where would she go anyway?

She closed her eyes while bouncing one knee. At some point, Cooper would have to go. She would wait. Through her eyelids she saw a burst of light and opened them. The larger log in the fireplace crackled as it caught fire. She could feel the heat now, and wished she could sit right in front of it. A large black iron pot hung from a metal rod that could swing over the fire—obviously the cabin's only stove.

"You can relax now, kids." Cooper added with a menacing smile. "No one can find us out here."

Alex wanted to say, 'Oh yeah,' but didn't.

"Not much on size, but it's a great hideaway. I even have a refrigerator, of sorts." He pointed to a rectangular piece of plywood on the floor. "That's my cold cellar. My fridge. That's where I put the stuff I need to keep cold. Why, you'd be surprised by what's down there."

Alex glanced at Robin. Her eye was swollen and turning black. He couldn't read her face—never could when she didn't want anyone to.

Cooper grimaced. "You kids are filthy. Can't stand kids, and filthy ones are worse. First sign of light, you'll take a swim in the lake out there," he said, nodding toward the door.

While Cooper rambled on, Marc looked for anything he could use as a weapon. He saw spider webs and dust everywhere—such a difference between this place and Cooper's house. He was surprised the man could handle it. He spotted a screwdriver and wrench hanging on nails next to the window. *Five steps*, he thought, *just five steps away.*

Cooper plucked a roll of gray duct tape hanging on a nail between the studs and told them to hold out their wrists. Reluctantly they held them up while he put fresh tape on them. He tore three more strips and covered each of their mouths. He placed the tape on the mantel, grabbed a lantern, and lifted the trap door. He propped a stick in the opening and descended below the floor. Alex looked at the others. If they could get to the trap door and slam it shut, they'd have him locked up.

Alex and Marc leaped off the bench, but Cooper suddenly shouted, "Sit! I can see you through the cracks in the floor!"

Marc didn't stop. He nearly reached the trap door when he heard Cooper's voice—almost a whisper.

"I can shoot right through the boards."

Marc was inches from the handle. All he had to do was kick the stick propping open the door and it would drop. Cooper would probably shoot him, but the others might get away—if they'd run. He could see Cooper's dark eyes watching him through a space between two floor boards.

"I told you I wouldn't make another mistake. I've been watching *you* the whole time."

Marc returned to the bench and slumped onto it. They were trapped. As trapped as Cooper could have been.

Marc was hungry and thirsty and tired. And by the looks of Robin's bouncing leg, she was desperate to go to the bathroom.

Alex closed his eyes and thought of all the things he would miss if Cooper killed them. He'd miss his mother and grandfather. School. Arrowhead hunting. And, like his father, he wouldn't grow old. He'd just assumed he'd go to college, get married to somebody like Allie, have kids and a house, and grow old and get that cool-looking sterling silver hair like his grandfather's. The room suddenly felt like a coffin.

He hoped his grandfather was tracking them and was out there somewhere closing in. He would be—if the trail Alex had marked was clear enough.

He looked at Robin. She was scared. Neither she nor Marc knew he had been marking the trail. There had been no way to tell them.

In his mind, he repeated the mantra for his grandfather. *U wo, Tunkaśila—Come, Grandpa. U wo, Tunkaśila. U wo, Tunkaśila.* Had he bent the branches enough? Was it too dark or too rainy? And the biggest worry of all, would his grandpa get there in time?

He tried to breathe slowly to calm himself, but his mind fired thoughts like bullets into the air, up to the spirits. *Please help Grandpa find us. Please.*

A heavy thud jarred him. His eyes snapped open. Cooper was still rummaging around the cellar. Alex couldn't imagine what he was up to, but it probably wasn't good. He tried to concentrate harder. *Hurry, Grandpa. Please hurry.*

When Kota reached level ground, he found himself in a stand of tall trees with low branches and bushes. If Alex had been there, why hadn't he left any marks. Kota reached for the flashlight in his belt, but it was gone. He remembered laying it on the ledge above the incline. He wanted to return for it, but time was of the essence. He moved on, running his fingers lightly over the ground from time to time, seeking footprints. He found them. Short strides. They were moving slower. He should be able to close in on them.

The moon suddenly peeked between the clouds, lighting his way. Its position in the sky told him it was past midnight. As it darted in and out of the clouds, he knew more light would also enable Cooper to see him. He would have to stay in the shadows.

Following the trail through the trees, he caught a scent. *Smoke! Was Cooper foolish enough to start a fire? It was like sending up smoke signals!* He sniffed again and followed the scent of burning wood.

He trotted along, increasing his pace, but he couldn't stop wondering about the smoke. *Was it a trap?* Lakota sometimes used fire as a diversion, or to stampede buffalo. *Was Cooper drawing him into an ambush? Was he watching him now?* Kota crouched low as he pulled out his knife. Through the trees, he noticed a cabin with a plume of smoke rising above it. *But that wasn't possible. There couldn't be a cabin in a national forest, unless he had entered private property. It was possible.*

Keeping his distance, he circled the cabin. *Not only was there a fire going, but there were lights. Surely Cooper was not stupid enough to create a lighthouse to draw attention to himself. It had to be a trap.* Kota had to know for sure before he made a move or he could jeopardize all their lives.

He searched the perimeter for anything suspicious, but found nothing. There were no recent footprints except on the north side where the entrance to the cabin faced Summer Lake.

After his careful search, Kota felt sure Cooper was not

in the woods. He stealthily climbed a tree near a side window. The branches were the right height to look inside, but he couldn't see anyone.

He slid down the tree and climbed up another that gave him a better angle and view. When he peered in, he was ecstatic to see the kids sitting together on a bench. Their backs were to him, and they were slumped and dirty, but they were alive!

He strained to see where Cooper was, but couldn't see him. *Was he in a corner?* He doubted it. At least one of the kids would be looking that way. Right now, they all seemed to be looking at the floor. Cooper might be outside after all, getting water, or watching him from one of the trees.

He stayed perfectly still and observed the trees around him. Nothing. He scanned the ground beneath him. Again, nothing. He steadied himself in the branches. His legs felt the strain of the night. Pieces of pine bark cracked off under the weight of his boots. He slipped a little, but caught himself by grabbing a sturdy limb.

Now it was a waiting game. He had to know where Cooper was. Anxious, moments passed, moments in which he became the tree, but he couldn't stay in the tree much longer. At over two hundred pounds, he was like an old bear, too big to be clinging to a tree for too long. It was time to take a chance.

He slid down the trunk, dropping the last few feet into a

silent crouch. *Become the forest.* In the stillness he heard an
owl hoot. Water sloshed on the shore. Something moved in
the grass to the right. He remained still. A four-legged. A
śiyo—a grouse—ambled through the brush. Good omen.
Critters wouldn't be afoot if someone else were there. Time
to make his move.

He cut a large bush to use as camouflage and crept closer to the cabin. With the bush as cover, he moved within two
feet of the window and looked inside. Still no sign of
Cooper. It didn't make sense. He looked up at the ceiling.
No loft. He doubted there was a basement in such a tiny
cabin.

He leaned back on his haunches to head for the lake
when he noticed the trap door propped open towards the
back of the cabin. A head appeared from below. He saw a
black beard, then the rest of a body. Cooper!

So where was the partner? Below? Cooper carried a gun
in one hand and potatoes and carrots in the crook of his
other arm. It was a cold cellar. The other man could be
down there.

Cooper placed the food on the floor in front of the fireplace, removed the iron pot from the hook, and faced the
kids with his gun pointing at them.

Kota didn't like it one bit. The man was a psychopath,
unpredictable. He wanted to crash through the door or window, but rejected the idea. First, the kids needed to know he

was outside. He cupped his hands around his mouth, caroled a couple of notes like a robin, and watched the kids for a reaction.

Sweat broke out on Robin's face. She had to go to the bathroom so bad and couldn't wait much longer. She tried to get up the nerve to ask if she could go outside, when she heard something. Something like—a bird call. It trilled again. It was a robin's carol. At night? *Kota!* Her eyes popped wide open and she jolted, bumping Alex in the process.

She started stomping the floor while Alex stared at her. He elbowed her as Cooper's eyes narrowed on them.

Robin kept stomping. Alex and Marc just stared at her.

With the boys' heads turned towards Robin, Kota could see the duct tape on their mouths. Their hands were probably taped as well. Possibly their feet.

When Cooper stomped across the floor with the gun, Kota was ready to spring.

Alex's heart pounded in his chest. He moved his hands across his lap and with one finger felt the outline of the tiny scissors in his pocket. Somehow, he had to get them out.

Cooper reached Robin and yanked the tape from her mouth.

"Yeowwwwww!" she shrieked, pressing the back of her hand to her lips.

Kota heard her and started for the window, but saw Cooper talking. He hunched back down to wait.

"What is it, pest?" Cooper barked, staring down at her.

"I've got to go *real* bad, Mister. I mean my bladder is going to explode all over this room if I don't go, *nowwww*."

"I'll bet you do, Red."

Kota tensed. He wanted to burst in and choke the man.

"I guess you can see there's no plumbing. No water except what's in the lake, so you'll have to go outside."

She nodded.

"So here's the deal. I'll let you go out, but you have to take that pot right there," he pointed to the hearth, "and fill it with water from the lake. Make sure you don't get the water from the same spot. Understand, kid?"

She nodded, causing her glasses to slide down her nose.

"It's only forty feet straight out that door," he said, pointing the gun.

Her eyes shifted to the door. The thought of getting out made her all tingly. Kota was out there. *What would he want her to do? How was he going to save them?*

"Let's make sure we're on the same page, Red."

Her bladder was throwing a party and she couldn't hold it much longer. She wanted to scream that Kota was outside and would get him, but couldn't. Kota hadn't rushed the cabin. He must need her to do something.

Cooper put his face into hers. "You're going to be outside all by yourself, right?"

His breath smelled like rotten meat. She recoiled.

"It'd be awfully tempting to run, now wouldn't it, Missy?"

Robin wasn't sure how to answer.

"I'm letting you do it because I know you'll come back." He pointed the gun at Alex's head.

Cooper continued. "If you don't come back, you'll never see your friends here again. At least you won't see them alive. Understand?"

She nodded, crossing and uncrossing her legs. "Please, mister, I gotta go *bad.*"

"Good," he said. "Just so we understand one another. Now, get the bucket and make it snappy."

Robin dashed across the room and tried to lift the iron pot but struggled with her taped wrists.

"Oh yeah," Cooper said. "Forgot that little detail."

He picked up a knife, and sliced the tape between her wrists. His hand moved so fast, her breath caught in her throat. She swallowed, grabbed the kettle, and headed for the door with the pot bumping against her legs as she shuffled across the floor. Before she left, she looked over her shoulder at Marc and Alex. They were watching her intently. *Did they think she wouldn't return?*

The Attack
✳ ✳ ✳ ✳ ✳ ✳

This was the break Kota had been waiting for. As Robin lumbered towards the lake with the iron pot, he slipped into the woods and crept through the trees on a parallel course.

A few feet from the lake, she dropped the pot and hurried to the water. The thought of snakes passed through her mind, but that didn't matter now. She splashed through the frigid water, pushing her legs forward and gasping as it inched up her body. The rocky bottom caused her to stumble and fall. Ignoring the cold, she pulled down her jeans and squatted in the water.

A bobcat cried somewhere in the forest. She quickly pulled up her jeans and shuffled around to face the trees. She'd heard there were bears out here, too. The skin on her back prickled. *Where was Kota?* In the sporadic moonlight, she scanned the thicket of trees, but couldn't see him anywhere. Maybe she'd been wrong about the bird call. After all, she'd been wrong about the frog, or so they said. At least she was outside now, but so were the bears, and bobcats, and whatever else—and her friends were inside with a gun to their heads.

Her body couldn't take much more tension and fear. She was tired and hungry and she didn't want to think anymore. She just wanted to curl up in a warm bed, go to sleep, and wake up to find it was all a bad dream.

Kota crept just inside the trees overhanging the water. His movement was limited by Cooper watching from the doorway.

"*Šišóka!*" he called softly.

"Kota!" she whispered in a rush, looking toward the trees. "Thank goodness—"

He cut her off. "Keep looking at the water. He is watching. Don't let on that I'm here. Don't look this way."

Robin looked down at the water again.

"What's he planning to do, *Šišóka?*"

"I don't know, Kota. He's crazy. I'm so glad you're here. I have to fill the pot with water. After that—who knows? But if I don't fill this pot and get back he's going to shoot Alex."

"Where's his partner?"

"Haven't seen him."

That was good news. "Fill the pot."

She got the pot from the shore and dragged it through the water near the trees where Kota hid. She floated the pot as she moved, then tilted it to let water run in. It filled and sank.

Kota grinned as she struggled with the pot. "Tell him it's too heavy."

"Okay."

Something brushed against her leg. She shrieked.

"What is it?" Cooper called out.

"Something's in the water!"

"Yeah, a wimp," he said. "Fill the pot."

"Are there snakes out here?" she whispered to Kota.

"No," he lied, "water's too cold for 'em."

She gripped the handle and tugged as hard as she could, but the pot didn't move an inch. She heaved repeatedly, but still it wouldn't budge.

"Tell him you need help," Kota said.

Holding onto the handle she yelled, "Mister. Mister!"

Cooper heard her call. "What now?"

"I can't lift it. With the water in it, it's too heavy."

Kota held his breath. He wanted the man to come out into the open.

Cooper scratched his temple with the barrel of the gun.

Under his breath, Kota muttered, "Come out, you—"

Cooper looked inside the cabin and said, "Hey, Mohammed! Get your butt off the bench and help her."

Marc sprang from the bench and hurried to Cooper with his hands up so he could cut the tape.

Cooper hesitated. "Now remember, I'll ice your friend over there if the two of you don't come back."

Marc quickly nodded.

Cooper got the knife from the shelf again, but hesitated. Instead, he stood in front of Marc rotating the handle in his hand.

Marc's stomach tightened.

Finally, Cooper cut the tape. Marc rubbed his wrists and turned to leave, but Cooper thrust his arm across the doorway and stopped him.

He glared at Marc. "Remember what I said."

Marc pulled the tape off his mouth. "I know. I'll be back."

While Cooper leaned against the doorjamb watching Marc, Alex contemplated what had happened. It was unbelievable that two of them had made it outside. He had a fleeting hope he would too, but Cooper would never let all three of them out at the same time. He had to think of something fast.

Cooper suddenly jerked around. "Stop it!"

Alex's breath caught in his throat. He hadn't realized his shoe was tapping nervously on the floor. He stopped and lowered his head.

Cooper looked out the door again.

From the corner of his eye, Alex saw him turn and knew this was his best chance to do something. He twisted his hand and strained against the tape to free the fingers of one hand. He tried to shove them into his pants pocket. But he couldn't get his fingers deep enough with his wrists taped. He slid his hand down the outside of the pocket and slowly edged the scissors to the top. He touched the metal handle with his little finger.

Cooper slapped a mosquito on the side of his neck.

Alex jumped and jerked his finger out, but Cooper didn't notice. He exhaled and slid his little finger back inside his pocket till he felt the scissors. He quickly pulled them out and tucked them under his leg on the bench.

Cooper still hadn't turned. He was too intent on watching Robin and Marc. But he would any second. Beads of sweat popped on Alex's forehead. He felt his cheeks suck in and out as he breathed hard under the tape. He slid his little finger under his leg, pulled the scissors out, and stuck them in his lap. While he watched Cooper, he bent his hand at a sharp angle and slipped his forefinger and thumb into the scissor rings. He worked the blades across the tough, fibrous tape. He pushed and snipped till his hand cramped. Finally, the tape gave.

Outside, Marc waded through the cold water to reach Robin. He whispered, "The guy's nuts. We've got to get Alex out and get out of here before he kills us."

Robin leaned closer to him. "Kota's here."

"No way!" He looked up.

"Don't look around. Look busy. Kota's hiding in the trees."

Marc needed to hear his voice. "Kota?"

"Here. Just look like you're trying to lift the pot."

"Boy am I glad you're here," Marc said, rotating the container. "Alex is inside."

"Cooper's watching," Kota said. "Act like you're trying to pick up the pot, but can't. Make him think it's still too heavy."

They did as he said. They stumbled and sloshed and splashed.

Cooper's hands went to his hips. "Don't tell me the two of you can't lift that kettle!"

"It's stuck to the bottom," Robin said.

"Yeah," Marc said. "Feels like it's stuck in the silt and won't release."

Kota just needed a little more time and he could have the knife in Cooper's heart, but he suddenly "knew" Alex was going to try something. There was no time now and his knife couldn't reach its mark from this distance. Seconds counted. If Cooper didn't come towards the lake soon, Kota would have to close the distance in the open, which would be risky with Cooper in the doorway holding a gun.

Kota kept his eyes fixed on him, pulling his knife from

the sheath. He gripped the end of the cold blade firmly in his right hand and readied it above his shoulder. Then he waited, watching for any sign of Cooper turning to Alex. As he breathed steadily in and out, he thought of Marc and Robin just feet away. They were out of the cabin and within his reach. *Should he pull them from harm's way before they wound up inside again with a killer? Saving two is better than the possibility of none. But could he sacrifice his grandson for the assured safety of Robin and Marc? What a predicament. If he grabbed the kids, Cooper would go for Alex and he couldn't risk losing—*

Cooper appeared startled and started to turn. Then a coffeepot smashed across his head.

There was no turning back now. Kota sprang from the trees like a panther and charged towards the cabin. Marc and Robin dropped into the water and huddled behind the iron pot as much as they could in case Cooper fired.

Cooper staggered against the door and steadied himself.

Kota ran, trying to close the distance he needed to throw his knife. Cooper lifted his gun and aimed at Alex.

Kota had no choice but to throw and pray it would hit its mark. He gave a screeching war cry that ripped through the dark like an arrow, then flung the knife with the strength of ten men.

The knife spun end over end, flickering in the moonlight as it whooshed through the air. Kota raced like a deer running for its life. His feet pounded the earth. His arms pumped like pistons propelling him faster.

The war cry stunned Cooper and his eyes and gun moved towards the sound. He saw flashes of metal. Before the image could register in his brain, the blade pierced his hand, pinning it to the door. The gun dropped, thumping to the porch and discharged.

Alex felt a sting-zing on the right side of his abdomen and went weak in the knees. He gripped his side and felt a finger-width hole in his jeans. He tilted back his hand, but saw no blood. Through the hole he saw the bent nail file. He looked back at Cooper and winced. Red blood oozed down the man's hand and onto his arm. Alex's eyes settled on the big knife nailing the hand to the door.

"Grandpa!" he said as Kota ran towards the cabin.

"Run, boy!" Kota yelled without taking his eyes off Cooper.

Alex sprang past Cooper, giving the gun a swift kick into the yard as he passed. He leaped from the porch and ran towards the lake.

Cooper pulled the knife from his hand, groaning as it popped free. He turned and saw the big Indian speeding towards him. *The gun! Where was the gun?* He quickly looked around. Gone. When he looked back, he was blinded by a handful of mud. He wiped his eyes with his sleeve as the Indian slammed into his midsection head first, knocking the breath out of him. He struggled to breathe, but the crazy Indian wouldn't stop. He pinned him against the door and beat his hand against the doorjamb over and over till the knife dropped and clattered to the porch. Then a forearm hit him across the throat. He dropped to the floor, gasping for air. His eyes settled on the knife just inches away. He snatched it and as the Indian grabbed him by the shoulders and whirled him around, he rammed the knife into his side. The Indian stiffened and slumped, then fell to the floor. Cooper then kicked him in the chest and shoved him off the porch.

The kids watched in horror as Kota hit the ground and rolled onto his back. The knife handle protruded from his body.

Alex jumped up, but Marc grabbed him in a bear-hug and pulled him into the bushes. With Kota hurt, they would be sitting ducks now and had to stay out of sight. Marc covered Alex's mouth and held him tight while he struggled to get loose.

Robin ran to them, parting the bushes enough to see Cooper head back into the cabin. Glass smashed and through the doorway she saw him sling kerosene from the lamp. He backed onto the porch, struck a match, and tossed it in.

He held his injured hand against his body and jumped from the porch. Behind him, a booming *whoosh* shattered the silence, turning night into day. Robin and the boys ducked. In seconds, the cabin was an inferno. Glass windowpanes popped, shattered, and clinked everywhere.

Another explosion sounded. The kids hit the ground again. This time, Marc covered his head and lost his grip on Alex. Before he knew it, Alex was running towards his grandfather. Marc rose to his knees and looked around. Cooper was nowhere in sight.

"Grandpa! Grandpa! Are you all right?" Alex ran faster than he ever had in his life and slid the last few feet, dropping to the ground beside Kota.

Kota's shirt was saturated with blood that reflected the golden flames. Alex watched the knife rise and fall as his grandfather labored to breathe. He wanted to scream out, but knew it wouldn't help.

Marc was at his side in seconds. "Shouldn't we," he motioned with his hands, "pull it out?"

Robin was right behind Marc and stopped at Kota's feet. He was unbelievably pale and the heat from the fire was intense. "I think so. Pull it out." Her cheeks were getting hotter. "And we need to get him away from the fire."

"I don't know." Alex's voice cracked. "Moving him might make it worse, might make him—bleed more."

Kota remained absolutely still.

"Grandpa!" There was no response. "Talk to me, Grandpa. Please! Tell us what to do. Should we pull out the knife?" Tears ran down Alex's cheeks.

Kota's eyes slowly half opened and closed. "Y-yes. And

p-pressure." The voice was so weak.

Alex looked at the knife and swallowed. He gripped the knife, but hesitated when his grandfather winced with pain. Robin couldn't understand why he hesitated. *What was wrong?* The knife had to come out. She pushed Alex aside and dropped to her knees. She gripped the knife with both hands, drew in a breath, and jerked it out as fast as she could. Kota's chest rose as the knife slid out, then settled.

"Ugh!" Marc said, covering his mouth with his hand.

Robin rocked back on her heels and stood with the knife still in her hand.

Alex scooted back to his grandfather's side and pressed on the wound.

"Alex, I think Robin's right about moving your grandpa. The fire could spread or something could explode. We don't know what he had in the basement. Let's slide him now, okay?"

The fire crackled. Light danced on their faces. Sweat trickled down Marc's face while he waited for Alex to respond.

"Guess you're right." Alex choked back tears. "But we have to be careful. Don't want him to bleed more."

Alex pressed on the wound while Marc and Robin grabbed Kota's feet and dragged him away from the fire. When he was a safe distance away, they stopped.

Alex said, "Grandpa! Are you okay?"

Kota opened his eyes again. "Where's—Cooper?"

"He ran into the woods," Marc told him, "back the way we came."

"Got to stop him." His voice was weaker. "Dangerous." He tried to get up, but Alex stopped him.

"Grandpa! You're not going anywhere. You'll kill yourself!"

"I'll go," Marc said. He swallowed real hard. "I'm fast and I can catch up with him."

Kota grabbed Marc's wrist. "No."

Robin looked at Kota's bloody clothes. His chest shuddered, then rose and dropped, and shuddered again. The life was draining out of him. She willed the air in her lungs to go to him and never return, because she didn't deserve it. She chewed her bottom lip, feeling helpless. It was all her fault! All of it! She was the one who took off in a huff that night on her bike. The one who had the flat tire. The one who stumbled across Cooper and his partner. The one who left her bike out there for them to trace. She was the one who brought the killer to their doorsteps. And *she* was the one who had to make things right!

Kota was right—Cooper had to be stopped and Kota couldn't do it. She didn't want Marc's life on her conscience and Alex was a basket case. Kota was getting restless and wouldn't relax till Cooper was found. There was only one answer. She had to stop Cooper.

She stared at the bloody knife in her hand, drew in a shaky breath, and took one last look at her friends bending over Kota. Tears rolled down her cheeks. She closed her eyes and prayed silently:

God, please don't let Kota die. He's a good man. Take me if you have to—I'm nothing—but don't let him die. I'll even be nice to Stanley. So just let him live.

Robin wiped her tears and shoved her glasses back in place. There would be no more tears. She looked over her shoulder at the woods. Cooper was out there—possibly watching now. She squeezed the grip of Kota's knife for a measure of courage, and began easing away from them while their attention was fixed on Kota.

Kota tried to get up. Alex gently pressed him down again.

"Stay together," Kota whispered. "Only chance."

With his eyes still closed, Kota said, "Robin."

Marc and Alex looked at one another, then turned to where Robin had stood.

"She's gone!" Marc gasped.

Alex closed his eyes tight. It was too much.

Marc tried to discern shapes in the trees. *What was Robin doing?* Sometimes she could be blinded by a task, like the night of their meeting when she left on her bike. *What was she going to do if she caught up with Cooper?* He looked around for the knife. It was gone too. He panicked.

If she tried to pull that knife on Cooper, he'd kill her in an instant. Somebody had to do something fast, or Robin was going to die.

He eased backwards, while Alex tended Kota. When he was far enough away he turned and sprinted into the trees.

Fifty feet into the woods he stopped. Everything was just dark shapes and shadows. And he was no Daniel Boone. He stood at the junction of two paths, but didn't know which to take. He kicked the ground in frustration, getting briars stuck to his ankle. He braced his hand against a tree to quickly pull them out.

When Robin got a short distance into the trees, she stopped to get her bearings. Up ahead was the stand of sycamores the way she had seen them when she checked the back trail. It was the right path.

Moonlight filtered through the branches and in the dim light she saw Kota's blood on the blade. She took a couple deep breaths, bent down to wipe off the blood and paused. This was Kota's blood. Warrior blood. It deserved better than being discarded in the dirt like toxic waste. She wished for his kind of courage, warrior courage, especially now.

She ran a finger down one side of the blade, easing Kota's drying blood onto her finger. She marked a line along her right cheekbone, then one across her left. She swiped the other side of the blade and marked a line down her nose and her chin. Now she wore Kota's warrior blood and would have his spirit. She stood, straightened, and felt taller.

She held the knife in the air and whispered, "Okay, Kota. I need your strength now. I need your courage and spirit. Be with me." Her heart began to race as she charged down the path.

Boards in the cabin crackled and creaked and began to collapse. The air was dense with smoke and embers. Alex covered his grandfather with his body to protect him from flying debris. He watched charred boards topple. He would never be able to look at a fire again, not even a match, without thinking of this moment. It was like watching something die and not being able to do anything—like with his grandfather. He turned to Marc, but his friend was gone.

"Marc?" he called weakly.

He and his grandfather were alone.

He sat back on his heels and ran his fingers through his hair. *What was happening? Would he ever see his friends alive again?* He looked down at his grandfather's ashen face and wondered if he was going to lose everything.

A Spider to the Rescue
✳ ✳ ✳ ✳ ✳ ✳

The sheriff sat in his squad car watching Bob Beekler approach him for the fourth time in less than an hour. The uppity conservation officer was a pain in the neck. He had enough on his mind without that guy bugging him every ten or fifteen minutes. A call came in on the radio as Beekler reached the side of the car. The sheriff gladly ignored him and answered it.

The *whomp-whomp-whomp* of helicopter blades came through loud and clear over the radio.

"Sheriff, this is Chopper 73. I have a visual of a fire in progress. I'm over the northeast quadrant of Kirk County Forest, due south of Summer Lake. Repeat. Fire in progress. Appears to be a small cabin. Over."

The sheriff grimaced, leaned his elbow on the window and pressed the button. "Chopper 73, this is Sheriff Jacobs, Jefferson County. Must be some mistake. There's no cabin on government land. Check your location. Over."

"Chopper 73 again. Government land or no, I have a visual on a cabin fire on the south bank of Summer Lake."

Bob hit the top of the car. "South bank? That's private land along the lake—backed up to the forest. There *is* a cabin there."

"Chopper 73 again. Lotta smoke down there, but I do see one man down and a kid with him."

Bob grabbed the sheriff's elbow. "Tell him to pick me up. I know the area and I was a Marine medic. Maybe I can tend to the injuries."

The sheriff jerked his elbow back. "This is *police* business so stay out of it."

"I can radio that pilot if I have to. Get him here now."

Alex coughed. The smoke was a problem now. It was drifting his way and occasionally obscuring the moon, making things darker. He prayed. When he finished he said, "Dad, I know you're up there. If you can, please help Robin and Marc. Keep them safe. And please—oh please don't let Grandpa die!"

The cabin was breathing fire and belching smoke. Against the dark woods, it looked like a dragon with tongues of fire.

He looked down at his grandfather. He was so still. Too still. He rubbed stinging sweat from his eyes when he heard a twig snap in the woods. He looked towards the bushes and

and felt he wasn't alone. He scooted closer to his grandfather, wondering whether Marc had found Robin—or whether Cooper had gotten them and had come after him.

He gently laid his head on his grandfather's chest. His heartbeat was weak. The rhythm flowed into his own body like a current through the centuries—centuries of Indian music and life and history and death. The cycle. He heard the beat of it all and closed his eyes.

Robin recognized the oaks on her left. Three of them growing together. They had been on the opposite side earlier when they came into the clearing. She was on the right path. She pushed her glasses back up and moved on.

As she walked, she turned the handle of Kota's knife over and over in her hand, feeling its rough leather texture on the haft. It felt heavy—and wrong. She walked a few more steps and practiced jabbing the knife. She couldn't imagine sticking it in a person, but when the time came, she would have to. She walked farther and raised the knife above her head and stabbed straight down. Then she sliced the air from side to side. None of it felt right.

Could she actually use the knife if she found Cooper? Her stomach felt queasy. She had the urge to toss the knife into the bushes, but decided not to. It could buy some time.

When she reached the incline, she slipped on the gravel, falling onto her knees and sending rocks rattling below.

She had to be more careful or she might fall and cut herself with the knife—or go flying over the edge.

The thorns in Marc's ankle bit like teeth. He pulled them out and when he straightened, noticed something thick and gooey on his hand. It had a coppery smell. He held his hand up in the moonlight filtering through the branches and saw the dark color. *Blood!* Cooper's? Or Robin's? There was no time. He had to try to find her before it was too late.

Alex listened to his grandfather's heartbeat while the fire crackled. He felt numb, and had the sinking feeling Robin and Marc were dead, or soon would be. Their lifeless bodies could be lying at the bottom of that black, rocky ravine—and he and his grandfather could be next.

His head seemed to pound—*ka-thump, ka-thump.* Then it changed to *whomp, whomp, whomp*—and it became louder. Then trees and bushes swayed, and dirt, leaves, and ash whirled in the air, pelting him in the face and stinging his eyes. The smell of ash went up his nose and his hair stood on end. It was like a tornado. He covered his grandfather's face. He looked up. Overhead was a helicopter. A blinding beam of light surrounded them like a glass jar over bugs.

"Grandpa! Grandpa! It's a helicopter! They've come for us!"

Kota didn't move. Above them, a gurney slowly dropped like a spider on its thread swaying in and out of the column of light.

"Grandpa, they're here. Hold on. I love you, Grandpa! Don't go with Dad."

A hand touched his shoulder. "It's okay, Alex. Stand back, so I can help him."

Alex wiped his face and said, "He looks soooo bad. He's going to die. I just know it."

The man patted his shoulder. "Let me take a look, Alex."

The man knew his name. Alex looked at his face. "Mr. Beekler?"

"I didn't know if you'd remember me," Bob said, feeling Kota's pulse. It was weak. Very weak. He saw the blood on Kota's shirt and ripped it open. When he saw the wound he stuffed it with cotton wads, then pulled the two-way radio from his belt and described Kota's condition.

He looked at Alex. "He still has a pulse. We'll have him at the hospital in minutes where he'll get the best medical care available."

"He's not going to die, is he?"

"Help me get him on the gurney."

They moved quickly. Bob strapped him in and straddled the gurney. He gripped the steel cable and told Alex to wait till he dropped the harness for him. He signaled the pilot to lift and the gurney rose into the sky.

Alex shielded his eyes from the wind and watched them disappear into the belly of the helicopter. Then a scream shattered the night. The sound was louder than the whirling helicopter blades and sent shivers up his back. *Robin!*

When Bob got the gurney into the helicopter, he lowered the harness back to the ground. Alex's heart beat harder as he watched it coming his way. Bob leaned out and yelled something through cupped hands. Alex reached for the rope when a second piercing scream rent the air. His eyes went to the woods, then back to his lifeline dangling before his eyes. He could finally get out of here. He gripped the straps, but hesitated to look over his shoulder once more. The sound had come from the overlook. He was certain of it. Could he abandon his friends? Were they even alive?

On the Edge
✳ ✳ ✳ ✳ ✳ ✳

By the time Cooper reached the overlook, he had lost a lot of blood and felt weak. His hand throbbed in a white-hot heat. Why not rest? He didn't have to worry about the old Indian and the kids now. The last thing they wanted was to tangle with ol' Coop again. And the police were no problem. He had eluded them and the dogs. He had heard a helicopter, but looking for him in these woods would be like shining a light in a haystack.

Looking back, he was a fool to have dragged the kids along. He should have wasted them when he had the chance. They only complicated everything. But, it didn't matter now because he was on his way to Costa Rica, where they'd never catch him.

Costa Rica! He loved the sound of it, the way it danced off his tongue. If he played his cards right, he'd be there tomorrow night. He just needed to rest a little now and rewrap his hand with the strips he was tearing from his T-shirt. Then he'd head for the fish camp, swipe a boat, and in no time, be down the Ohio River. He'd see about getting his money later.

He looked out over the treetops for the last time. Across the landscape he saw the bright glow of the cabin fire and froze. That fire would draw forest rangers like moths. He had to get to the fish camp as soon as possible.

He quickly tied the strips of fabric from his shirt and cursed the old Indian. *Where did he come from anyway? Was he some kind of bloodhound?* He remembered the kid yelling, "Grandpa." Of all the rotten luck. He had to kidnap a kid whose grandfather was an Indian scout.

He heard gravel chink on the path below. *A deer?* The woods were thick with them. He strained to look down the trail and saw something glimmer. *A silver leaf maple swaying in the moonlight?*

Cooper kept his eyes fixed on the trail. There it was again. Definitely a glimmer, like a reflection on glass. *Glasses?* That pesky girl with those infernal glasses? He had to be hallucinating. After all, he'd lost a lot of blood. But there she was, climbing closer. She couldn't be stupid enough to come after him. He'd kill her this time for sure.

He scrambled to his feet. Maybe his mind was playing tricks on him. He blinked and looked again. But there she was. *Where were the other kids? Ahead of her?* He spun around, becoming a little dizzy. He had lost too much blood and knew he couldn't fight or outrun all three of them. They'd be like a pack of dogs bringing down a wounded deer. His best chance would be to surprise the pesky girl, here at the top of the knoll and shove her off. Then he'd deal with any others. He retreated into the trees as she approached, but he stumbled on some gravel, making it clink across the rocky surface.

Robin heard the clink on the rock ledge up ahead and halted. It had to be Cooper at the overlook. She hurried the last few feet and stopped.

She waited. *Melt into the night,* Kota would say. She waited for another sound. But all she heard were crickets and left-over rain dripping from the leaves. She studied the trees and the bushes and saw something metallic lying on the rock surface. Clouds parted and a sprinkle of moonlight spilled onto the rock revealing a flashlight. She wondered if Cooper knew it was there. If only she knew exactly where he was.

Cooper waited still as a post for her to cross the clearing. But time was running out. The brat could wait all night. He had to do something.

He bent down, felt around for a rock, and tossed it to his left to make her think he was there. With luck, she would move across the ledge in front of him. He waited, but she didn't budge. *Was she waiting for the others?* He felt light-headed and swayed into the brush next to him, startling a tree of bats that took flight in a black cloud of fluttering wings that obscured the sparse moonlight. He ducked and gasped an obscenity.

Robin heard a pebble and saw bats suddenly flutter from a bush. Then she heard him curse. Now she knew exactly where he was—directly behind the flashlight. He must not have seen it. She also realized he didn't have another gun or he wouldn't be hiding.

She tightened her grip on Kota's knife. The handle felt big for her hand and heavier than when she first picked it up. There was a whirring sound far off, but she had to focus on Cooper now. She stepped into the clearing.

Cooper's heart beat double-time when he saw her tiptoe onto the ledge. He drew in a breath, screamed like a banshee and bolted towards her.

Marc was at the base of the hill when he heard the flurry of bats and could tell it came from the top of the knoll. Someone must have spooked them. He charged up the incline as fast as he could. Halfway up he heard a scream and saw Cooper burst from the bushes toward Robin.

Robin was startled by a war cry and froze as Cooper

sprang onto the ledge and slipped on the flashlight. His feet flew out from under him, and she ducked out of the way. There was a loud crack as he hit the rock. When she looked up, his legs were hanging off the ledge and he was clawing desperately to climb back onto solid ground.

She had to stop him. She tightened her grip on the knife and raised her hand high above her head. In seconds, everything that had happened flashed through her mind. Seth's murder, being kidnapped—and slapped. The poisoned land and corn, and how she and her friends almost died. Rage roared through her and she raised the knife to plunge it into his hand reaching across the rock.

"Please—help me," he begged. His shoes scraped the rock wall.

She hesitated. He looked frightened, like a poor little animal. She couldn't stand it. She laid down the knife and eased onto her belly and chest. When she reached for his hand, she got only bandages, and he slid a few more inches over the edge. He suddenly grabbed her wrist and his weight started dragging her toward the edge. She struggled to free herself, but he entangled the fingers of his injured hand in her loose hair.

She screamed in pain from the weight of the dangling man. From her vantage point above him, she could see right down into the black abyss. Her stomach felt as if it leaped into her throat.

Her glasses fell from her face, hitting him in the forehead. He shook his head, flinging them into the darkness like sweat. She felt dizzy and nauseated and puked sour-smelling liquid in his face.

He spit and sputtered and cursed, but held on.

She slid another inch. She pressed the palms of her hands harder against the gritty rock surface to keep from sliding. Wind blew in her face as her shoulders inched over the edge. Cooper jerked to get a better grip. Her body teetered at the point of no return. She felt herself falling, going over the side with him and she knew she was going to die.

As she squeezed her eyes shut, two hands suddenly grasped her ankles and held her fast. The rock edge pressed into her stomach and her arms and legs felt like taffy being pulled in two directions, but she wasn't falling!

"Hang on, Robin!" Marc yelled. "I've got you!" He dug in his heels. Then he leaned backwards for leverage and pulled with all his might. He strained, but Robin seemed glued to the spot. He took a few quick breaths and pulled again with all his might, but she wouldn't budge. Then his foot slipped and Robin slid forward.

"I can't—hold—much longer," he said between grunts.

Blood rushed to her head and she could barely breathe from the pain. She had to think of something. Her mind scrambled for possibilities.

Marc shifted to the right and her hip pressed onto the knife. She slid her free hand along the rock and wrapped her fingers around the handle. Without hesitation, she raised the knife above Cooper.

Cooper felt a shift. He looked up and saw something flash in the moonlight. She had the Indian's knife raised high in the air. *She was going to cut off his hand!* He jerked on her hair to stop her, but it just made her eyes narrow with determination and in one slicing motion she brought down the knife. The blade sliced through the air and chopped off her hair above his entangled fingers. His arm swung free and his body swayed like a pendulum while he still gripped the fistful of hair in one hand and held her sweating wrist in the other. He looked back up at Robin. Her eyes were wild. Her jagged hair danced in the wind, framing her blood-streaked face. For a brief moment, he saw the image, or maybe the ghost, of that Indian back at the cabin. He jolted before he realized it, loosening his grip.

Robin felt his grip falter and jerked back her hand. Cooper seemed motionless, his face, awash with terror, his diamond earring twinkling in the moonlight. His hand slid from her wrist as if it had been greased. She was mesmerized as he fell like a stone, his arms reaching for help. Then he was gone.

A piercing scream filled the air and reverberated off the cliff wall as Marc pulled her backwards across the bumpy surface and toppled over. A muffled thump sounded below.

Still stunned, she was staring at the rock's edge when a large crow rose from below and hovered above her. Her breath caught in her throat. It flapped its wings and something shiny sparkled in its beak. *A diamond?* Confused, she watched as the bird rose high enough to silhouette against the large, round moon and vanish as if swallowed by it.

She closed her eyes and wondered about all that happened. She looked back at the moon. It was nestled amongst the clouds, as normal as ever, as if tucked in for the night.

She scooted back, laid her head on Marc's chest and was comforted by the steady lud-dub of his heart. Her neck hurt so bad she didn't know if she could lift her head again.

"Cooper's gone. Cooper's gone," she whispered and closed her eyes.

A beam of light passed between Robin and Marc and settled on her, penetrating her eyelids like sunshine on a window shade. Her fingers tightened on Kota's knife.

"Robin!"

She forced her eyes to open and beyond the light saw Alex's outline. She went limp again as she felt him stare at her. She must look a sight. Her hair was chopped off, her eye felt swollen, and her face was streaked with blood.

"What happened to you?" Alex whispered.

Her lips were dry and hard to move, so she said nothing.

He looked around. "Where's Cooper?"

Her eyes moved from him to the edge of the rock.

"He fell over?" Alex guessed.

She tried to nod, but her neck was in too much pain.

"No way!" He shook his head. "The guy was like Freddy Krueger." He walked to the edge and shone the light down below. When he returned, he said, "Did *you* do it?"

She laid her forearm across her eyes and didn't answer. Finally, she asked, "How's Kota?"

"They've flown him across the river to a hospital in Louisville. Bob came in a helicopter to rescue him."

"My Uncle Bob?" She sat up slowly, bracing her neck with both hands, the knife still clutched in one. "He went with Kota?"

"Yeah, but he'll be back for us. Grandpa should be okay."

Alex looked down at Marc. "Hey, Bud."

Marc mumbled, but didn't move.

"He okay?"

"Pretty tired," she said.

Alex gestured towards her face. "What's with all the smudges?"

"Long story, but it's over—I hope." Her eyes went from the edge of the cliff to the trees behind her where Cooper had hidden.

Alex set Bob's flashlight on the ground to light the area. "Your uncle shouldn't be long."

She brushed dirt from her palms. "I couldn't do it, Alex. After everything he did to us, and to Seth and Kota, I still couldn't kill him when I had the chance." She stared at the knife in the dim light.

She saw Alex look at the drop-off. He probably wanted to ask what happened, but she was too tired to explain it all.

"Robin, it's probably a good thing you didn't. You might have regretted it for the rest of your life." He wiped his dirty hand on his jeans. "Grandpa once told me that most everyone has the potential for good and for evil. You're just someone who has all the good and no evil."

She studied her raw, bony knuckles and pointed to the edge. "What does that say about him?"

"He was pure evil. A real pirate, if you ask me. Now he's where he belongs. But it took all your goodness and courage to get him there—where he can't ever hurt anybody else."

Robin looked up at the moon. It was as round and brilliant as a porcelain plate. "Remember the moon, Alex? The upside-down one with the curse?"

He nodded.

"I thought it was all superstition." She rubbed the chill from her arms. "But it's true. And when Cooper fell, well, a crow appeared, and I think it had a diamond in its beak. Then it just vanished—into the moon."

He stared at her, then looked up at the moon. An owl hooted nearby. He looked over his shoulder into the trees behind them. When he looked ahead again, he asked, "Do you think it's really over?"

"Cooper's gone," she said. "Kota's going to be okay and we'll be going home soon."

He studied the streaks across her cheeks. "And," he said, "this time the pirates left and the Indians stayed."

"But what's going to happen in the next quarter century when the upside-down moon comes back?"

"I don't know. Maybe it won't," he said.

Marc's voice startled them. "Where's that other guy— the Buster guy?"

Alex snatched the flashlight, fumbled with the switch, and turned it off.

Alex was the first to hear the *whomp, whomp, whomp* of the helicopter. He turned on the flashlight and stood waving at it. The copter veered their way and hovered, swirling trees and particles into the air while its beam of light encircled them.

"It's your Uncle Bob, Robin," Alex said.

Bob descended in a harness. When he reached the ground and saw Robin's face, he hugged her tight. "What in the world happened out here?"

She buried her face in his shirt.

"It's okay," he said, patting her. "We can talk later. For now, let's just get you out of here." He pried her hand open and took the knife away. In a matter of seconds, she was strapped in the harness and rising to the helicopter.

When all were on board, the pilot radioed police headquarters and told them to notify the parents that the kids were okay and on their way to Kirk Memorial Hospital to be treated for dehydration, minor cuts and bruises, and bug bites. He was told Kota was coming out of surgery and should make a full recovery.

Robin was treated at the hospital and fitted with a neck brace. When she was released, her mother drove her to the nearest restaurant where she ordered Robin the biggest breakfast on the menu. While they waited for the food, Robin jabbed the root beer float with her straw and asked, "Where's Stanley?"

"Stanley," her mother said, clearing her throat, "won't be with us anymore."

Robin stopped jabbing the drink. "What happened?"

Her mother seemed to look for the words in her cup. "It turns out he might have been mixed up with the two men who killed Seth. When everything came out, he left town. No one's seen him since."

"Wow!" Cracker crumbs fell from Robin's lips. "You're not making this up, are you, Mom?"

"No, Honey. Apparently, Stanley was the inside man."

"Stanley? Really?"

"I don't know why I married him in the first place. And if I ever lost you—well, I just don't know what I'd do." A tear slid down her face.

"Mom, we don't need him. We've got each other. Just you and me—like it used to be."

Her mother looked down and started fidgeting with her silverware.

"There's something else, isn't there, Mom?"

She nodded. "Yes, honey—I'm pregnant."

A Special Kind of Courage

✳ ✳ ✳ ✳ ✳ ✳

On Sunday, Robin and Marc went to Alex's house to see Kota, eat pizza, and watch a movie. Robin's hair had been cut in a style copied from a picture in a teen magazine. She would get new glasses the following Monday, but her eye was still black. Marc told her it was a good thing because when Brad saw her eye and heard what she did, he'll think twice about messing with her.

They talked about her stepfather's involvement and how he skipped town. Robin told them that going through that horrible ordeal was worth it to be rid of him. She also told them about Sonny Dyer stopping by and giving her a new red bicycle for helping find his father's killers. She told them he was really nice and would be having dinner with her mother tonight. She decided not to say anything about her mother's secret, not yet, anyway. She also wondered how Stanley, or Sonny, would react when they found out.

Kota opened the door and Rags ran into the den. His tail

wagged and he stood on his hind feet to sniff his approval of Robin's hair. She patted him and fished two dog chews from her pocket. He quickly snatched them and gobbled them up.

Kota smiled at all of them as Karen helped him into the easy chair.

"Hey. There are my heroes." His arm was taped to his side and bruises darkened his right cheek.

"That's a real shiner you've got there, *Šišóka*." He tucked strands of her shortened, layered hair behind her ear. "What you did out there in the forest was very brave."

Her face felt hot. She knew she was blushing. "I'm not brave, Kota. I'm not—"

Kota held up a hand to stop her. "My people believe everyone has it in them to be brave. They just need a chance to learn they can be. You were each given that chance. You each displayed a special kind of courage. Lakota warriors were called Braves for a reason and that's how I think of you."

"Marc, you were loyal and had the courage to risk your life to save a friend. Alex, you believe you did nothing in that dark night, but you tended me as life was draining out of me. That is such an act of love. It is very difficult to look death in the eyes and stay fast."

Kota turned to Robin. "You, *Šišóka*, tracked a killer alone and risked your life to save others. And you learned

284

you do not have the killing spirit. Instead, you would harm yourself before you would harm others." He smiled while shaking his head at her.

"You wonder why *Wakan Tanka* gave you such brilliant red hair? Well, the Lakota believe red is the color of honor." He lifted her chin with the crook of his finger. "Now when you look in the mirror you will be reminded of how brave you were. And how proud Seth is of you. And if you stay on the Red Road, you will be able to face and do anything."

Glossary

Please note:

The author does not profess to be educated in Lakota languages of which there are seven subgroups. These subgroups are known as The Seven Fires or The Seven Council Fires. It is these groups that account for slight differences in terms that some readers may notice. The terms used in this story are Oglala Lakota. Crazy Horse, the great Lakota leader, was Oglala.

Ahpe (ah-PAY) wait

Hanhepi wi (hahñ-HAY-pee wee) moon

Hunhunhe (hooñ-hooñ-HAY) man's expression of sorrow

Iho (ee-HO) term to get attention

Istima (ee-SHTEE-mah) sleep

Mihunka (mee-HOOÑ-kah) my brother, literally translated
"my chosen relative"

Mitakoja (mee-TAH-ko-jah) my grandson

Nagi (NAH-ghee) spiritual self

Šišóka (shee-sho-KAH) a robin

Śiyo (shee-YO) a grouse

Tatanka (tah-TAHÑ-kah) a buffalo

Tunkaśila (toon-KAH-shee-lah) grandfather

U wo (OO wō) come

Wakan Tanka (wah-KAHÑ tahñ-KAH) the Great Spirit

Wasu (wah-SOO) snow seeds, hail

Wicaśa Okinihan (wee-CHAH-shah oh-KEE-nee-hahñ) an honorable
and respected individual

Resources

Beebe Hill, Ruth. *Hanta Yo: An American Saga*. New York: Doubleday & Company, Inc., 1979.

Eliopulos, Louis N. *Death Investigator's Handbook*. Boulder: Paladin Press, 1993.

Marshall, III, Joseph M. *The Lakota Way: Stories and Lessons for Living*. New York: Penguin Books, 2001.

White Hat, Sr., Albert. *Reading and Writing the Lakota Language*. Salt Lake City: The University of Utah Press, 1999.